THE
LITTLE LAME PRINCE

Hope Dunlap '09

THE LITTLE LAME PRINCE

Dinah Mulock Craik
Illustrated by Hope Dunlop

Derrydale Books
New York • Avenel, New Jersey

 First published in 1993 by Derrydale Books, distributed by Outlet Book Company, Inc., a Random House Company, 40 Engelhard Avenue, Avenel, New Jersey 07001

Random House
New York • Toronto • London • Sydney • Auckland
Designed by Eileen Rosenthal
Printed and bound in the Singapore

Library of Congress Cataloging-in-Publication Data
Craik, Dinah Maria Mulock, 1826–1887. The little lame prince / by Dinah Mulock Craik: illustrated by Hope Dunlap. p. cm. Summary: A young crippled prince must reclaim his kingdom from his evil uncle, with the help of a magic cape from his godmother.
ISBN 0-517-08484-8 : $8.99 [1. Fairy tales. 2. Physically handicapped—Fiction.] I. Dunlap, Hope, ill. II. Title.
[PZ8.C845Li 1993] [E]—dc20 92-37665 CIP AC

8 7 6 5 4 3 2 1

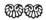

Introduction

WELCOME TO NOMANSLAND, a place much like many others. It is a pretty country of beautiful mountains and flower-strewn meadows, of gamboling lambs and chirping birds. The children, like children everywhere, laugh and cry, play and study, and sometimes quarrel with each other. Although most of the grownups here are good and kind, there are some who you'll meet who are not every nice.

Nomansland is a magical place. For, in addition to children and grownups, there are fairies here. One, in particular, can cast the most wonderful spells. You'll meet Prince Dolor, too. He's a very special boy who, although he cannot walk, does have some amazing adventures with his traveling cloak.

Dinah Mulock Craik wrote this book in 1875, more than one hundred years ago. The story, which has been read by many generations of children, is as wonderful today as it was when it was first written.

Now turn the page and enter an enchanted land where strange and marvelous things can happen.

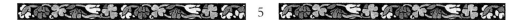

THE LITTLE LAME PRINCE

Chapter One

Yes, he was the most beautiful prince that ever was born. Of course, being a prince, people said this, but it was true besides. When he looked at the candle, his eyes had an expression of earnest inquiry quite startling in a newborn baby. His nose—there was not much of it certainly, but what there was seemed an aquiline shape. His complexion was a charming, healthy purple. He was round and fat, straight-limbed and long—in fact, a splendid baby, and everybody was exceedingly proud of him. Especially his father and mother, the king and queen of Nomansland, who had waited for him during their happy reign of ten years—now made happier than ever, to themselves and their subjects, by the appearance of a son and heir.

The only person who was not quite happy was the king's brother, the heir-presumptive, who would have been king one day, had the baby not been born. But as His Majesty was very kind to him, and even rather sorry for him—insomuch that at the queen's request he gave him a dukedom almost as big as a county—the crown prince, as he was called, tried to seem pleased too; and let us hope he succeeded.

The prince's christening was to be a grand affair. According to the custom of the country, there were chosen for him four-and-twenty godfathers and godmothers, who each had to give him a name, and promise to do their utmost for him. When he came of age, he himself had to choose the name—and the godfather or godmother—that he liked best, for the rest of his days.

Meantime, all was rejoicing. Subscriptions were made among the rich to give pleasure to the poor. There were dinners in town halls for the working men; tea parties in the streets for their wives; and milk and bun feasts for the children in the schoolrooms. For Nomansland, though it cannot be pointed out on books, any map, or read about in any history, was much like our own country or many other countries.

As for the palace—which was no different from other palaces—it was clean "turned out of the windows," as people say, with the preparations going on. The only quiet place in it was the room which, though the prince was six weeks old, his mother the queen had never left. Nobody said she was ill, however. It would have been so inconvenient. And since she said nothing about it herself, but lay pale and placid, giving no trouble to anybody, nobody thought much about her. All the world was absorbed in admiring the baby.

The christening day came at last, and it was as lovely as the prince himself. All the people in the palace were lovely, too—or thought themselves so, in the elegant new clothes that the queen, who thought of everybody, had taken care to give them, from the ladies-in-waiting down to the little kitchenmaid, who looked at herself in her pink cotton gown and thought that there never was such a pretty girl as she.

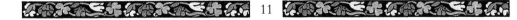

By six in the morning all the royal household had dressed itself in its very best. And then the little prince was dressed in his best—his magnificent christening robe, which proceeding His Royal Highness did not like at all, but kicked and screamed like any common baby. When he had calmed down a little, they carried him to be looked at by the queen his mother, who, though her royal robes had been brought and laid upon the bed, was, as everybody well knew, quite unable to rise and put them on.

She admired her baby very much. She kissed him and blessed him, and lay looking at him, as she did for hours sometimes, when he was placed beside her fast asleep. Then she gave him up with a gentle smile, and saying she hoped he would be very good, that it would be a very nice christening, and all the guests would enjoy themselves, she turned peacefully over on her bed, saying nothing more to anybody. The queen, whose name was Dolorez, was a very uncomplaining person.

Everything went on exactly as if she had been present. All, even the king himself, had grown used to her absence, for she was not strong, and for years had not joined in any gaieties. She always did her royal duties, but as to pleasures, they could go on quite well without her, or it seemed so. The company arrived: great and notable persons from this and neighboring countries; also the four-and-twenty godfathers and godmothers, who had been chosen with care, as the people who would be most useful to His Royal Highness, should he ever want friends, which did not seem likely.

They came, walking two and two, with their coronets on their heads—being dukes and duchesses, princes and princesses, or the like. They all kissed the child, and pronounced the name that each had given him. Then the four-and-twenty names were shouted out with great energy by six heralds, one after the other. Afterward the names were written down, to be preserved in the state records, in readiness for the next time they were wanted, which would be either on His Royal Highness's coronation or at his funeral. Soon the ceremony was over, and everybody was satisfied, except, perhaps, the little prince himself, who moaned faintly under his christening robes, which nearly smothered him.

In truth, though very few knew, the prince in coming to the chapel

had met with a slight disaster. His nurse—not his ordinary one, but the state nursemaid, an elegant and fashionable young lady of rank, whose duty it was to carry him to and from the chapel, had been so occupied in arranging her train with one hand, while she held the baby with the other, that she stumbled and let him fall, just at the foot of the marble staircase. To be sure, she picked him up again the next minute, and the accident was so slight it seemed hardly worth speaking of. Consequently, nobody did speak of it. The baby had turned deadly pale but did not cry, so no person a step or two behind could discover anything wrong. Afterward, even if he had moaned, the silver trumpets were loud enough to drown out his voice. It would have been a pity to let anything trouble such a day of felicity.

So, after a minute's pause, the procession had moved on. Such a procession! There were the heralds in blue and silver, pages in crimson and gold, and a troop of little girls in dazzling white, carrying baskets of flowers, which they strewed all the way before the nurse and child. Finally, there were the four-and-twenty godfathers and godmothers, as proud as possible, and so splendid to look at that they would have quite extinguished their small godson—merely a heap of lace and muslin with

Hope Dunlap

a baby face inside—had it not been for a canopy of white satin and ostrich feathers, which was held over him wherever he was carried.

Thus, with the sun shining on them through the painted windows, they stood. The king and his train were on one side, the prince and his attendants on the other, as pretty a sight as ever was seen out of fairyland.

"It's just like fairyland," whispered the eldest little girl to the next eldest, as she shook the last rose out of her basket. "And I think the only thing the prince wants now is a fairy godmother."

"Does he?" said a shrill but soft and not unpleasant voice behind. And there was seen among the group of children somebody—not a child, yet no bigger than a child. It was somebody whom no one had seen before, and who certainly had not been invited, for she had no christening clothes on.

She was a little old woman dressed all in gray—gray gown, gray hooded cloak, of a material excessively fine and a tint that seemed perpetually changing, like the gray of an evening sky. Her hair was gray, and her eyes were also. Even her complexion had a soft gray shadow over it. But there was nothing unpleasant about her, and her smile was as sweet and childlike as the prince's own, which stole over his pale little face the instant she came near enough to touch him.

"Take care. Don't let the baby fall again."

The grand young lady nurse started, flushing angrily. "Who spoke to me? How did anybody know? I mean, what business has anybody—?" Then, frightened, but still speaking in a much sharper tone than young ladies of rank are in the habit of speaking—"Old woman, you will be kind enough not to say 'the baby,' but 'the prince.' Keep away. His Royal Highness is just going to sleep."

"Nevertheless, I must kiss him. I am his godmother."

"You!" cried the elegant lady nurse.

"You!" repeated all the gentlemen and ladies in waiting.

"You!!!" echoed the heralds and pages—and they began to blow the silver trumpets, to stop all further conversation.

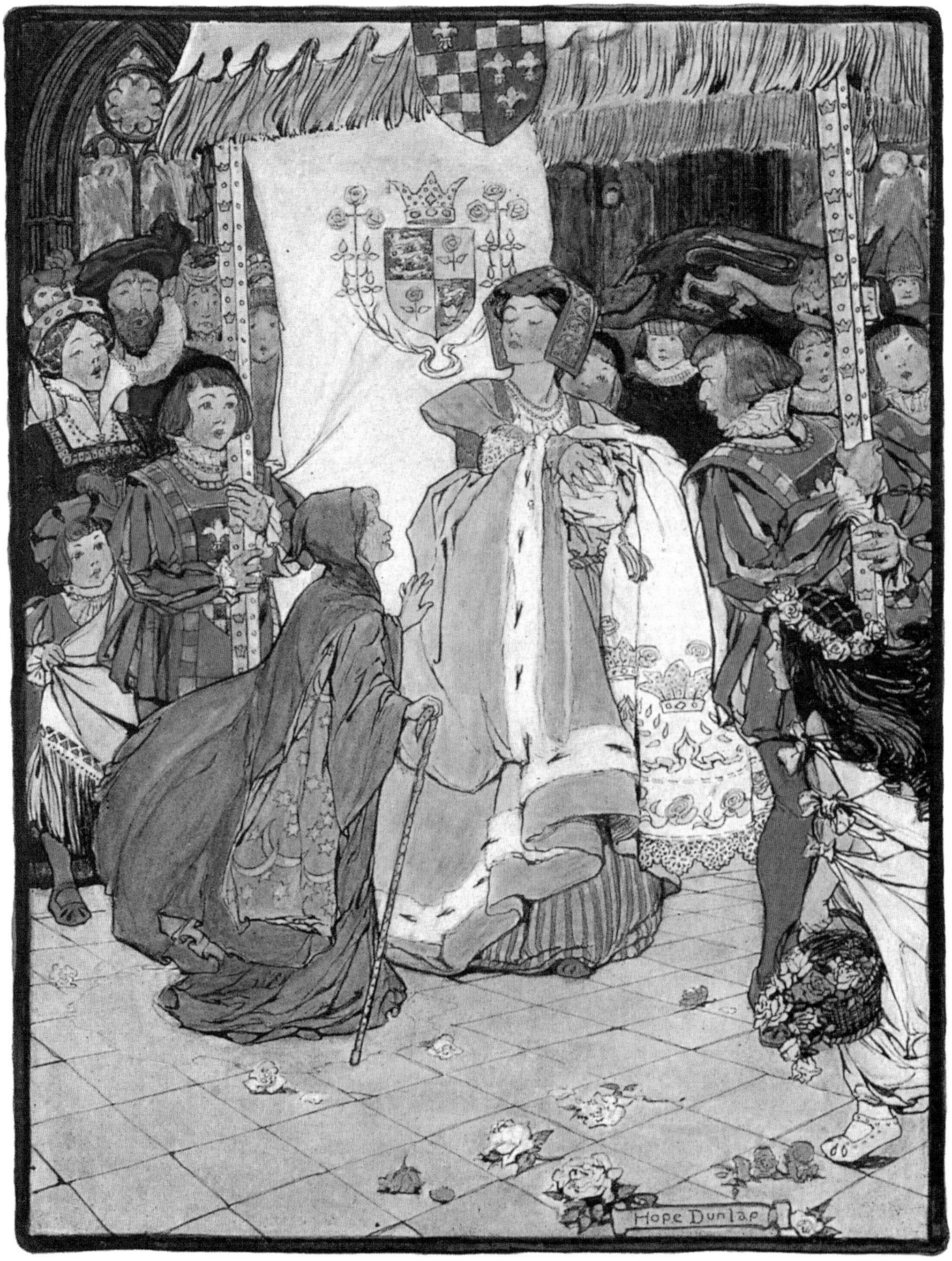
Hope Dunlap

The prince's procession formed itself for returning. The king and his train had already moved off toward the palace. But, on the topmost step of the marble stairs, stood, right in front of all, the little old woman clothed in gray.

She stretched herself on tiptoe with the help of her stick, and gave the little prince three kisses.

"This is intolerable," cried the young lady nurse, wiping the kisses off rapidly with her lace handkerchief. "Such an insult to His Royal Highness. Take yourself out of the way, old woman, or the king shall be informed immediately."

"The king knows nothing of me, more's the pity," replied the old woman with an indifferent air, as if she thought the loss was more on His Majesty's side than hers. "My friend in the palace is the king's wife."

"Kings' wives are called queens," said the lady nurse, with a contemptuous air.

"You are right," replied the old woman. "Nevertheless, I know Her Majesty well, and I love her and her child. And since you dropped him on the marble stairs"—this she said in a mysterious whisper, which made the young lady tremble in spite of her anger—"I choose to take him for my own. I am his godmother, ready to help him whenever he wants me."

"You help him!" cried all the group, breaking into shouts of laughter, to which the little old woman paid not the slightest attention. Her soft gray eyes were fixed on the prince, who seemed to answer to the look, smiling again and again in causeless, aimless fashion, as babies do smile.

"His Majesty must hear of this," said a gentleman-in-waiting.

"His Majesty will hear quite enough news in a minute or two," said the old woman sadly. And again stretching up to the little prince, she kissed him on the forehead solemnly.

"Be called by a new name that nobody has ever thought of. Be Prince Dolor, in memory of your mother Dolorez."

"In memory of!" Everybody started at the ominous phrase, and also at a most terrible breach of etiquette that the old woman had committed. In Nomansland, neither the king nor the queen were supposed to have any Christian name at all. They dropped it on their coronation day, and it was never mentioned again until it was engraved on their coffins when they died.

"Old woman, you are exceedingly ill-bred," cried the eldest lady-in-waiting, much horrified. "How you could know the fact passes my comprehension. But even if you did not know it, how dared you presume to hint that her most gracious Majesty is called Dolorez?"

"*Was* called Dolorez," said the old woman with a tender solemnity.

The first gentleman, called the Gold-stick-in-waiting, raised it to strike her, and all the rest stretched out their hands to seize her. But the gray mantle melted from between their fingers like air. And, before anybody had time to do anything more, there came a heavy, muffled, startling sound.

The great bell of the palace—the bell that was only heard on the death of some of royal family, and for as many times as he or she was years old—began to toll. They listened, mute and horrorstricken. Someone counted: One—two—three—four—up to nine and twenty. Just the queen's age.

It was, indeed, the queen. Her Majesty was dead! In the midst of the festivities she had slipped away, out of her new happiness and her old sufferings, neither few nor small. Sending away her women to see the sight—at least, they said afterward, in excuse, that she had done so, and it was very like her to do it—she had turned with her face to the window, from where could just be seen the tops of the distant mountains—the Beautiful Mountains, as they were called—where she was born. So gazing, she had quietly died.

When the little prince was carried back to his mother's room, there was no mother to kiss him. And, though he did not know it, there would be for him no mother's kiss any more.

As for his godmother—the little old woman in gray who called herself so—whether she melted into air, like her gown when they touched it, or whether she flew out of the chapel window, or slipped through the doorway among the bewildered crowd, nobody knew. Nobody ever thought about her.

Only the nurse, the ordinary one, coming out of the prince's nursery in the middle of the night in search of a cordial to quiet his continual moans, saw, sitting in the doorway, something that she would have thought a mere shadow, had she not seen shining out of it two eyes, gray and soft and sweet. She put her hand before her own, screaming loudly. When she took them away, the old woman was gone.

Chapter Two

Everybody was very kind to the poor little prince. He had a magnificent nursery, and a regular suite of attendants, and was treated with the greatest respect and state. Nobody was allowed to talk to him in silly baby language, or dandle him, or, above all, to kiss him, though, perhaps, some people did it when no one was looking, for he was such a sweet baby that it was difficult not to.

It could not be said that the prince missed his mother; children of his age cannot do that. But somehow after she died everything seemed to go wrong with him. From a beautiful baby he became sickly and pale, seeming to have almost ceased growing, especially in his legs, which had been so fat and strong. But after the day of his christening they withered and shrank. He no longer kicked them out either in passion or play, and when, as he got to be nearly a year old, his nurse tried to make him stand upon them, he only tumbled down.

This happened so many times that at last people began to talk about it. A prince, and not able to stand on his own legs! What a dreadful thing! What a misfortune for the country!

Rather a misfortune for him too, poor little boy! But nobody seemed to think of that. And when, after a while, his health revived, and the old bright look came back to his sweet little face, and his body grew larger and stronger, though still his legs remained the same, people continued to speak of him in whispers, and with grave shakes of the head. Everybody knew, though nobody said it, that something, impossible to guess what, was not quite right with the poor little prince.

Of course, nobody hinted this to the king his father. It does not do to tell great people anything unpleasant. And besides, His Majesty took very little notice of his son, or of his other affairs, beyond the necessary duties of his kingdom. People had said he would not miss the queen at all, she having been so long an invalid. But he did. After her death he never was quite the same. He established himself in her empty rooms, the only rooms in the palace from where the Beautiful Mountains could be seen. And he was often observed looking at them as if he thought she had flown there, and that his longing could bring her back again. And by a curious coincidence, which nobody dared inquire into, he desired that the prince might be called, not by any of the four-and-twenty grand names given him by his godfathers and godmothers, but by the identical name mentioned by the little old woman in gray—Dolor, after his mother Dolorez.

Once a week, according to established state custom, the prince, dressed in his very best, was brought to the king his father for half an hour. But His Majesty was generally too ill and too melancholy to pay much attention to the child.

Only once, when he and the crown prince, who was exceedingly attentive to his royal brother, were sitting together, with Prince Dolor playing in a corner of the room, dragging himself about with his arms rather than his legs, and sometimes trying feebly to crawl from one chair to another, it seemed to strike the father that all was not right with his son.

"How old is His Royal Highness?" he suddenly said to the nurse.

"Two years, three months, and five days, please Your Majesty."

"It does not please me," said the king with a sigh. "He ought to be far more forward than he is now, ought he not, brother? You, who have so many children, must know. Is there not something wrong about him?"

"Oh, no," said the crown prince, exchanging meaningful looks with the nurse, who did not understand at all, but stood frightened and trem-

bling with the tears in her eyes. "Nothing to make Your Majesty at all uneasy. No doubt His Royal Highness will outgrow it in time."

"Outgrow—what?"

"A slight delicacy—ahem!—in the spine. Something inherited, perhaps, from his dear mother."

"Ah, she was always delicate, but she was the sweetest woman that ever lived. Come here, my little son."

And as the prince turned round upon his father a small, sweet, grave face—so like his mother's—His Majesty the King smiled and held out his arms. But when the boy came to him, not running like a boy, but wriggling awkwardly along the floor, the royal countenance clouded.

"I ought to have been told of this. It is terrible—terrible! And for a prince, too! Send for all the doctors in my kingdom immediately."

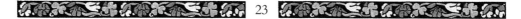

They came, and each gave a different opinion, and ordered a different mode of treatment. The only thing they agreed on was what had been pretty well known before: that the prince must have been hurt when he was an infant—let fall, perhaps, so as to injure his spine and lower limbs. Did nobody remember?

No, nobody. Indignantly, all the nurses denied that any such accident had happened, was possible to have happened, until the faithful country nurse recollected that it really had happened, on the day of the christening. For her unluckily good memory all the others scolded her so severely that she had no peace, and soon after, by the influence of the young lady nurse who carried the baby that fatal day, and who was a distant relative of the crown prince, being his wife's second cousin once removed, the poor woman was pensioned off, sent to the Beautiful Mountains, from where she came, with orders to remain there for the rest of her days.

But of all this the king knew nothing. Indeed, after the first shock of finding out that his son could not walk, and seemed never likely to walk, he interfered very little concerning him. The whole thing was too painful, and His Majesty had never liked painful things. Sometimes he inquired after Prince Dolor, and they told him His Royal Highness was going on as well as could be expected, which really was the case. For after worrying over the poor child and perplexing themselves with one remedy after another, the crown prince, not wishing to offend any of the differing doctors, had proposed leaving him to nature. And nature, the safest doctor of all, had come to his help, and done her best. He could not walk, it is true. His limbs were mere useless additions to his body, but the body itself was strong and sound. And his face was the same as ever—just his mother's face, one of the sweetest in the world!

Even the king, indifferent as he was, sometimes looked at the little fellow with sad tenderness, noticing how cleverly he learned to crawl, and swing himself about with his arms, so that in his own awkward way he was as active in motion as most children of his age.

"Poor little man! He does his best, and he is not unhappy; not half so unhappy as I, brother," said the king to the crown prince, who was more constant than ever in his attendance upon the sick monarch. "If anything should befall me, I have appointed you as regent. In case of my death, you will take care of my poor little boy?"

"Certainly, certainly, but do not let us imagine any such misfortune. I assure Your Majesty—everybody will assure you—that it is not in the least likely."

He knew, however, and everybody knew, that it was likely, and soon after it actually did happen. The king died, as suddenly and quietly as the queen had done—indeed, in her very room and bed. Prince Dolor was left without either father or mother.

He was more than a prince now, though. He was a king. In Nomansland, as in other countries, the people were struck with grief one day and revived the next. "The king is dead—long live the king!" was the cry that rang through the nation, and almost before his late Majesty had been laid beside the queen in their splendid mausoleum, crowds came thronging from all parts of the royal palace, eager to see the new monarch.

They did see him—the prince regent took care they should—sitting on the floor of the council chamber, sucking his thumb! And when one of the gentlemen-in-waiting lifted him up and carried him—fancy, carrying a king!—to the chair of state, and put the crown on his head, he shook it off again, it was so heavy and uncomfortable. Sliding down to the foot of the throne, he began playing with the golden lions that supported it, stroking their paws and putting his tiny fingers into their eyes, and laughing—laughing as if he had at last found something to amuse him.

"There's a fine king for you!" said the first lord-in-waiting, a friend of the prince regent's (the crown prince that used to be, who, in the deepest mourning, stood silently beside the throne of his young nephew. He was a handsome man, very grand and clever looking). "What a king! A boy who can never stand to receive his subjects, never walk in processions, who, to the last day of his life, will have to be carried about like a baby. Very unfortunate!"

"Exceedingly unfortunate," repeated the second lord. "It is always

bad for a nation when its king is a child, but such a child—a permanent cripple, if not worse."

"Let us hope not worse," said the first lord in a very hopeless tone, and looking toward the regent, who stood erect and pretended to hear nothing. "Well, let us hope for the best and be prepared for the worst. In the meantime——"

"I swear," said the crown prince, coming forward and kissing the hilt of his sword—"I swear to perform my duties as regent, to take all care of His Royal Highness—His Majesty, I mean," with a grand bow to the little child, who laughed innocently back again. "And I will do my humble best to govern the country. Still, if the country has the slightest objection——"

But the crown prince being generalissimo, and having the whole army at his beck and call, so that he could have begun a civil war in no time, the country had, of course, not the slightest objection.

So the king and queen slept together in peace, and Prince Dolor reigned over the land—that is, his uncle did. And everybody said what a fortunate thing it was for the poor little prince to have such a clever uncle

to take care of him. All things went on as usual. Indeed, after the regent had brought his wife and her seven sons, and established them in the palace, things went on rather better than usual. For they gave such splendid entertainments and made the capital so lively that trade revived, and the country was said to be more flourishing than it had been for a century.

Whenever the regent and his sons appeared, they were received with shouts—"Long live the crown prince!" "Long live the royal family!" And, in truth, they were very fine children, all seven of them, and made a great show when they rode out together on seven beautiful horses, one height above another, down to the youngest, on his tiny black pony, no bigger than a large dog.

As for the other child, His Royal Highness Prince Dolor—for somehow people soon ceased to call him His Majesty, which seemed such a ridiculous title for a poor little fellow, a helpless cripple, with only head and trunk, and no legs to speak of—he was seen very seldom by anybody.

Sometimes, people daring enough to peer over the high wall of the palace garden noticed there, carried in a footman's arms, or drawn in a chair, or left to play on the grass, often with nobody to mind him, a pretty little boy, with a bright intelligent face, and large melancholy eyes—no, not exactly melancholy, for they were his mother's, and she was by no means sad-minded, but thoughtful and dreamy. They rather perplexed people, those childish eyes. They were so exceedingly innocent and yet so penetrating. If anybody did a wrong thing, told a lie for instance, they would turn round with such a grave silent surprise—the child never talked much—that every naughty person in the palace was rather afraid of Prince Dolor.

He could not help it, and perhaps he did not even know it, being no better a child than many other children, but there was something about him which made bad people sorry, and grumbling people ashamed of themselves, and ill-natured people gentle and kind. Perhaps it was because they were touched to see a poor little fellow who did not in the least know what had befallen him, or that lay before him, living his baby life as happy as the day was long. Thus, whether or not he was good himself, the sight of him and his affliction made other people good, and, above all, made everybody love him. So much so, that his uncle, the regent, began to feel a little uncomfortable.

Now, uncles in general are usually very excellent people, and very convenient to boys and girls. This "cruel uncle" was, undoubtedly, an exception.

He did not mean to be cruel. If anybody had called him so, he would have resented it extremely. He would have said that what he did was done entirely for the good of the country. But he was a man who had been always accustomed to consider himself first and foremost, believing that whatever he wanted was sure to be right, and, therefore, he ought to have it. So he tried to get it, and he got it too, as people like him very often do. Whether they enjoy it when they have it is another question.

Therefore, he went one day to the council chamber, determined to make a speech and inform the ministers and the country at large that the young king was in failing health, and that it would be advisable to send him for a time to the Beautiful Mountains. Whether he really meant to do this, or whether it occurred to him afterward that there would be an easier way of attaining his great desire, the crown of Nomansland, is a point that is difficult to decide.

But soon after, when he had obtained an order in council to send the king away—which was done in great state, with a guard of honor composed of two whole regiments of soldiers—the nation learned, without much surprise, that the poor little prince—nobody ever called him king now—had gone on a much longer journey than to the Beautiful Mountains. He had fallen ill on the road and died within a few hours—at least so declared the physician in attendance and the nurse who had been sent to take care of him. They brought his coffin back in great state, and buried it in the mausoleum with his parents.

So Prince Dolor was seen no more. The country went into deep mourning for him and then forgot him, and his uncle reigned in his stead. That illustrious personage accepted his crown with great decorum, and wore it with great dignity, to the last. But whether he enjoyed it or not, there is no evidence to show.

Chapter Three

And what of the little lame prince, whom everybody seemed so easily to have forgotten?

Not everybody. There were a few kind souls, mothers of families, who had heard this sad story, and some servants about the palace, who had been familiar with his sweet ways—these many a time sighed and said, "Poor Prince Dolor!" Or, looking at the Beautiful Mountains, which were visible all over Nomansland, though few people ever visited them, "Well, perhaps His Royal Highness is better where he is than even there."

They did not know—indeed, hardly anybody did know—that beyond the mountains, between them and the sea, lay a tract of country, barren, level, bare, except for short, stunted grass, and here and there a patch of tiny flowers. Not a bush—not a tree—not a resting place for bird or beast was in that dreary plain. In summer, the sunshine fell upon it hour after hour with a blinding glare. In winter, the winds and rains swept over it unhindered, and the snow came down, steadily, noiselessly, covering it from end to end in one great white sheet, which lay for days and weeks unmarked by a single footprint.

Not a pleasant place to live—and nobody did live there, apparently. The only sign that human creatures had ever been near the spot, was one large round tower that rose up in the center of the plain, and might be seen all over it—if there had been anybody to see, which there never was. It rose right up out of the ground, as if it had grown of itself, like a

mushroom. But it was not at all mushroomlike. On the contrary, it was very solidly built. It was circular, of very firm brickwork, with neither doors nor windows, until near the top, there were some slits in the wall, through which it might be possible to creep in or look out. Its height was nearly a hundred feet high, and it had a battlemented parapet, showing sharp against the sky.

Since the plain was quite desolate—almost like a desert, only without sand—and led to nowhere except the still more desolate seacoast, nobody ever crossed it. Whatever mystery there was about the tower, it and the sky and the plain kept their secret to themselves.

It was a very great secret indeed—a state secret—which none but so clever a man as the present king of Nomansland would ever have thought of. How he carried it out, undiscovered, nobody knew. People said, long afterward, that it was by means of a gang of condemned criminals, who were set to work, and executed immediately after they had done, so that nobody knew anything, or in the least suspected the real fact.

And what was the fact? This tower, which seemed a mere mass of masonry, utterly forsaken, and uninhabited, was not so at all. Within twenty feet of the top, some ingenious architect had planned a perfect little house, divided into four rooms. By making skylights, and a few slits in the walls for windows, and raising a peaked roof which was hidden by the parapet, here was a complete dwelling. It was eighty feet from the ground, and as inaccessible as a rook's nest on the top of a tree.

It was a charming place to live in if you once got up there and never wanted to come down again.

Inside—though nobody could have looked inside except a bird, and hardly even a bird flew past that lonely tower—inside it was furnished with all the comfort and elegance imaginable. These were lots of books and toys, and everything that the heart of a child could desire. For its only inhabitant, except a nurse of course, was a poor little solitary child.

One winter night, when all the plain was white with moonlight, there was seen crossing it a great tall black horse, ridden by a man also big and wearing a black cloak, carrying before him on the saddle a woman and a child. The woman—she had a sad, fierce look, and no wonder, for she was a criminal under sentence of death, whose sentence had been changed to almost as severe a punishment. She was to inhabit the lonely tower with the child, and was allowed to live as long as the child lived—longer. This, in order that she might take the utmost care of him. For those who put him there were equally afraid of his dying and of his living. And yet he was only a little gentle boy, with a sweet sleepy smile—he had been very tired with his long journey—and clinging arms, which held tight to the man's neck, for he was rather frightened, and the face looked kindly at him. And he was very helpless, with his poor small shriveled legs, which could neither stand nor run away. For the little forlorn boy was Prince Dolor.

He had not been dead at all—or buried either. His grand funeral had

been a mere pretense. A wax figure having been put in his place, while he himself was spirited away under charge of these two, the condemned woman and the tall man. The man was deaf and could not speak, so he could neither tell nor repeat anything.

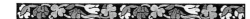

When they reached the foot of the tower, there was a light enough to see a huge chain dangling from the parapet, but dangling only halfway. The man took from his saddlebag a kind of ladder, arranged in pieces like a puzzle, fitted it together and lifted it up to meet the chain. Then he mounted to the top of the tower, and slung from it a kind of chair, in which the woman and the child placed themselves and were drawn up, never to come down again as long as they lived. Leaving them there, the man descended the ladder, took it to pieces again and packed it in his pack, mounted the horse, and disappeared across the plain.

Every month the woman and the child would watch for him, appearing like a speck in the distance. He tied his horse to the foot of the tower and climbed it, as before, laden with provisions and many other things. He always saw the prince, so as to make sure that the child was alive and well, and then went away until the following month.

While his first childhood lasted, Prince Dolor was happy enough. He had every luxury that even a prince could need, and the one thing wanting—love, never having known, he did not miss. His nurse was very kind to him, though she was a wicked woman. But either she had not been quite so wicked as people said, or she grew better as the result of being shut up continually with a little innocent child, who was dependent upon her for every comfort and pleasure of his life.

It was not an unhappy life. There was nobody to tease or ill use him, and he was never ill. He played about from room to room—there were four rooms—parlor, kitchen, his nurse's bedroom, and his own. He learned to crawl like a fly, and to jump like a frog, and to run about on all fours almost as fast as a puppy. In fact, he was very much like a puppy or a kitten, as thoughtless and as merry—scarcely ever cross, though sometimes a little weary. As he grew older, he occasionally liked to be quiet for a while, and then he would sit at the slits of windows—which were much bigger than they looked from the bottom of the tower—and watch the sky above and the ground below, with the storms sweeping over and the sunshine coming and going, and the shadows of the clouds running races across the empty plain.

By and by he began to learn lessons—not that his nurse had been ordered to teach him, but she did it partly to amuse herself. She was not a stupid woman, and Prince Dolor was by no means a stupid boy, so they got on very well, and his continual entreaty "What can I do? What can you find me to do?" stopped, at least for an hour or two in the day.

It was a dull life, but he had never known any other. Anyway, he remembered no other and he did not pity himself at all, at least not for a long time, until he grew to be quite a big little boy, and could read easily. Then he suddenly took to books, which the deaf man brought him from time to time. The books were very interesting. They told him of things in the outside world, and filled him with an intense longing to see it.

From this time a change came over the boy. He began to look sad and thin, and to shut himself up for hours without speaking. For his nurse hardly spoke, and whatever questions he asked beyond their ordinary daily life she never answered. She had, indeed, been forbidden, on pain of death, to tell him anything about himself, who he was or what he might have been. He knew he was Prince Dolor, because she always addressed him as "my prince," and "Your Royal Highness," but what a prince was he had not the least idea. He had no idea of anything in the world, except what he found in his books.

He sat one day surrounded by them, having built them up around him like a little castle wall. He had been reading them half the day, but feeling all the while that to read about things that you never can see is like hearing about a beautiful dinner while you are starving. For almost the first time in his life he grew melancholy. His hands fell on his lap. He sat gazing out of the window slit at the view outside, the view he had looked at every day of his life, and might look at for endless days more.

It was not a very cheerful view—just the plain and the sky—but he liked it. He used to think, if he could only fly out of that window, up to the sky or down to the plain, how nice it would be! Perhaps when he died—his nurse had told him once in anger that he would never leave the tower until he died—he might be able to do this. Not that he understood much what dying meant, but it must be a change, and any change seemed to him a blessing.

"And I wish I had somebody to tell me all about it, about that and many other things. Somebody that would be fond of me, like my poor white kitten."

Here the tears came into his eyes, for the boy's one friend, the one interest of his life, had been a little white kitten, which the man, kindly smiling, once took out of his pocket and gave him—the only living creature Prince Dolor had ever seen. For four weeks the kitten was his constant plaything and companion, until one moonlight night it took a fancy for wandering, climbed onto the parapet of the tower, dropped over, and disappeared. It was not killed, he hoped, for cats have nine lives. Indeed, he almost fancied he saw it pick itself up and scamper away, but he never caught sight of it again.

"Yes, I wish I had something better than a kitten—a person, a real live person, who would be fond of me and kind to me. Oh, I want somebody—dreadfully, dreadfully!"

As he spoke, there sounded behind him a slight tap-tap-tap, as of a stick or a cane, and twisting himself around, he saw nothing either frightening or ugly, but still exceedingly curious. A little woman, no bigger than he might himself have been, had his legs grown like those of other children. But she was not a child. She was an old woman. Her hair was gray, and her dress was gray, and there was a gray shadow over her wherever she moved. But she had the sweetest smile, the prettiest hands, and when she spoke it was in the softest voice imaginable.

"My dear little boy"—and dropping her cane, the only bright and rich thing about her, she laid those two tiny hands on his shoulders—"my own little boy, I could not come to you until you had said you wanted me, but now you do want me, and here I am."

"And you are very welcome, madam," replied the prince, trying to speak politely, as princes always did in books, "and I am exceedingly obliged to you. May I ask who you are? Perhaps my mother?" For he knew that little boys usually had a mother, and had occasionally wondered what had become of his own.

"No," said the visitor, with a tender, half-sad smile, smoothing back the hair from his forehead, and looking right into his eyes. "No, I am not your mother, though she was a dear friend of mine, and you are as like her as ever you can be."

Hope Dunlap

"Will you tell her to come and see me then?"

"She cannot, but I dare say she knows all about you. And she loves you very much—and so do I. And I want to help you all I can, my poor little boy."

"Why do you call me poor?" asked Prince Dolor in surprise.

The little old woman glanced down at his legs and feet, which he did not know were different from those of other children, and then at his sweet, bright face, which, though he knew not that either, was exceedingly different from many children's faces, which are often so fretful, cross, sullen. She smiled. "I beg your pardon, my prince," said she.

"Yes, I am a prince, and my name is Dolor. Will you tell me yours, madam?"

The little old woman laughed like a chime of silver bells.

"I have not got a name—or rather, I have so many names that I don't know which to choose. However, it was I who gave you yours, and you will belong to me all your days. I am your godmother."

"Hurrah!" cried the little prince. "I am glad I belong to you, for I like you very much. Will you come and play with me?"

So they sat down together and played. By and by they began to talk.

"Are you very bored here?" asked the little old woman.

"Not particularly, thank you, Godmother. I have plenty to eat and drink, and my lessons to do, and my books to read—lots of books."

"And you want nothing?"

"Nothing. Yes—perhaps—if you please, Godmother, could you bring me just one more thing?"

"What sort of thing?"

"A little boy to play with."

The old woman looked very sad. "Just the thing, alas, which I cannot give you. My child, I cannot alter your lot in any way, but I can help you to bear it."

"Thank you. But why do you talk of bearing it? I have nothing to bear."

"My poor little man!" said the old woman in the very tenderest tone of her tender voice. "Kiss me!"

"What is kissing?" asked the wondering child.

His godmother took him in her arms and embraced him many times. By and by he kissed her back again—at first awkwardly and shyly, then with all the strength of his warm little heart.

"You are better to cuddle than even my white kitten, I think. Promise me that you will never go away."

"I must, but I will leave a present behind me—something as good as myself to amuse you—something that will take you wherever you want to go, and show you all that you wish to see."

"What is it?"

"A traveling cloak."

The prince's face fell. "I don't want a cloak, for I never go out. Sometimes nurse hoists me onto the roof, and carries me round by the parapet, but that is all. I can't walk, you know, as she does."

"The more reason why you should ride; and besides, this traveling cloak . . ."

"Hush!—she's coming."

There sounded outside the room door a heavy step and a grumpy voice, and rattle of plates and dishes.

"It's my nurse, and she is bringing my dinner; but I don't want dinner at all—I only want you. Will her coming drive you away, Godmother?"

"Perhaps, but only for a little. Never mind. All the bolts and bars in the world couldn't keep me out. I'd fly in at the window, or down through the chimney. Only wish for me, and I will come."

"Thank you," said Prince Dolor, but almost in a whisper, for he was very uneasy at what might happen next. His nurse and his godmother—what would they say to one another? How would they look at one another? Two such different faces, one, harsh-lined, sullen, cross, and sad, the other, sweet, and bright and calm.

When the door was flung open, Prince Dolor shut his eyes, trembling all over. Opening them again, he saw he need fear nothing. His lovely old godmother had melted away just like the rainbow out of the sky, as he had watched it many a time. Nobody but his nurse was in the room.

"What a muddle Your Royal Highness is sitting in," she said sharply. "Such a heap of untidy books. And what's this rubbish?" kicking a little bundle that lay beside them.

"Oh, nothing, nothing—give it me!" cried the prince, and darting after it, he hid it under his shirt, and then pushed it quickly into his pocket. Rubbish as it was, it was left in the place where she had sat, and might be something belonging to her—his dear, kind godmother, whom already he loved with all his lonely, tender, passionate heart.

It was, though he did not know this, his wonderful traveling cloak.

Chapter Four

On the outside it was the commonest looking bundle imaginable—shabby and small. And the instant Prince Dolor touched it, it grew smaller still, dwindling down till he could put it in his trousers pocket, like a handkerchief rolled up into a ball. He did this at once, for fear his nurse should see it, and kept it there all day—all night, too. It was not until after his next morning's lessons that he had an opportunity to examine his treasure.

When he did, it seemed no treasure at all, but a mere piece of cloth—circular in form, dark green in color, that is, if it had any color at all, being so worn and shabby, though not dirty. It had a split cut to the center, forming a round hole for the neck—and that was all its shape; the shape, in fact, of those cloaks that in South America are called ponchos—very simple, but most graceful and convenient.

Prince Dolor had never seen anything like it. In spite of his disappointment he examined it curiously, spread it out on the floor, then arranged it on his shoulders. It felt very warm and comfortable, but it was so exceedingly shabby—the only shabby thing that the prince had ever seen in his life.

"And what use will it be to me?" said he sadly. "I have no need of outdoor clothes, since I never go out. Why was this given to me, I wonder? And what in the world am I to do with it? She must be a rather funny person, this dear godmother of mine."

Nevertheless, because she was his godmother, and had given him the cloak, he folded it carefully and put it away, poor and shabby as it was, hiding it in a safe corner of his toy cupboard, which his nurse never meddled with. He did not want her to find it, or to laugh at it, or at his godmother—as he felt sure she would, if she knew everything.

There it lay, and by and by he forgot all about it. Indeed, being but a child, and not seeing her again, he almost forgot his sweet old godmother, or thought of her only as he did of the angels or fairies that he read of in his books, and of her visit as if it had been a mere dream.

There were times, certainly, when he recalled her; on early mornings like that morning when she appeared beside him, and late evenings, when the gray twilight reminded him of the color of her hair and her pretty soft garments; above all, when, waking in the middle of the night, with the stars peering in at his window, or the moonlight shining across his little

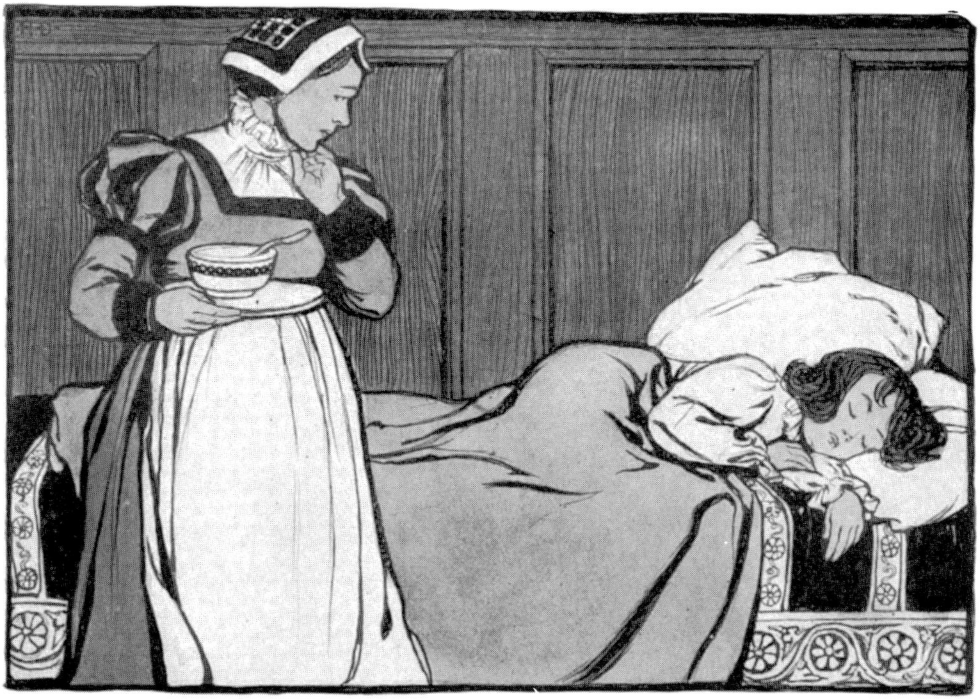

bed, he would not have been surprised to see her standing beside it, looking at him with those beautiful tender eyes, which seemed to have a comfort in them different from anything he had ever known.

But she never came, and gradually she slipped out of his memory—only a boy's memory, after all. And then something happened that made him remember her, and want her as he had never wanted anything before.

Prince Dolor fell ill. He caught—his nurse could not tell how—a complaint common to the people of Nomansland, called the doldrums, as unpleasant as measles or any other complaint. It made him restless, cross, and disagreeable. Even when he was a little better, he was too weak to enjoy anything, but lay all day long on his sofa, worrying his nurse extremely. In her intense terror lest he might die, she fidgeted about him more and more. At last, seeing he really was getting well, she left him to himself—which he was most glad of, in spite of his boredom. There he lay, alone, quite alone.

Now and then there came over him an irritable fit, in which he longed to get up and do something, or go somewhere; he would have liked to imitate his white kitten—jump down from the tower and run away, taking the chance of whatever might happen.

Only one thing, alas! was likely to happen; for the kitten, he remembered, had four active legs, while he——

I wonder what my godmother meant when she looked at my legs and sighed so bitterly? I wonder why I can't walk straight and steady like my nurse? Only I wouldn't like to have her great noisy, clumping shoes. Still, it would be very nice to move about quickly—perhaps to fly, like a bird, like that string of birds I saw the other day skimming across the sky one after the other.

These were the passage birds, the only living creatures that ever crossed the lonely plain. He had been very interested in them, wondering whence they came and whither they were going.

How nice it must be to be a bird, the prince thought to himself. If legs are no good, why cannot one have wings? People have wings when they die—perhaps. I wish I was dead, that I do. I am so tired, so tired, and nobody cares for me. Nobody ever did care for me, except perhaps my godmother. Godmother, dear, have you quite forsaken me?

He stretched himself wearily, gathered himself up, and dropped his head upon his heads. As he did so, he felt somebody kiss him at the back of his neck, and turning, found that he was resting, not on the sofa pillows, but on the warm shoulder of the little old woman.

How glad he was to see her! How he looked into her kind eyes, and felt her hands, to see if she were all real and alive! Then he put both his arms round her neck, and kissed her as if he would never stop kissing!

"Stop, stop!" she cried, pretending to be smothered. "I see you have not forgotten my teachings. Kissing is a good thing—in moderation. Only, just let me have breath to speak one word."

"A dozen!" he said.

"Well, then, tell me all that has happened to you since I saw you—or rather, since you saw me, which is quite a different thing."

"Nothing has happened. Nothing ever does happen to me," answered the prince dolefully.

"And are you very bored, my boy?"

"So bored that I was just thinking whether I could not jump down to the bottom of the tower like my white kitten."

"Don't do that, not being a white kitten."

"I wish I were! I wish I were anything but what I am!"

"And you can't make yourself any different, nor can I do it either. You must be content to stay just what you are."

The little old woman said this very firmly, but gently, too, with her arms around his neck, and her lips on his forehead. It was the first time the boy had ever heard anyone talk like this, and he looked up in surprise, but not in pain, for her sweet manner softened the hardness of her words.

"Now, my prince—for you are a prince, and must behave as such—let us see what we can do. Let's see how much I can do for you, or show you how to do for yourself. Where is your traveling cloak?"

Prince Dolor blushed. "I—I put it away in the cupboard. I suppose it is there still."

"You have never used it. You dislike it?"

He hesitated, not wishing to be impolite. "Don't you think it's—just a little old and shabby, for a prince?"

The old woman laughed long and loud, though very sweetly.

"Prince, indeed! Why, if all the princes in world craved for it, they couldn't get it, unless I gave it to them. Old and shabby! It's the most valuable thing imaginable! Very few ever have it. But I thought I would give it to you, because—because you are different from other people."

"Am I?" said the prince, and looked first with curiosity, then with a sort of anxiety, into his godmother's face, which was sad and grave, with slow tears beginning to steal down her cheeks.

She touched his poor little legs. "These are not like those of other little boys."

"Indeed! My nurse never told me that."

"Very likely not. But it is time you were told, and I tell you because I love you."

"Tell me what, dear Godmother?"

"That you will never be able to walk, or run, or jump, or play, that your life will be quite different than most people's lives. But it may be a very happy life for all that. Do not be afraid."

"I am not afraid," said the boy, but he turned very pale, and his lips began to quiver, though he did not actually cry. He was too old for that, and, perhaps, too proud.

Though not wholly understanding, he began dimly to guess what his godmother meant. He had never seen any real live boys, but he had seen pictures of them running and jumping, which he had admired and tried hard to imitate, but always failed. Now he began to understand why he failed, and that he always should fail—that, in fact, he was not like other little boys; and it was of no use his wishing to do as they did, and play as they played, even if he had had them to play with. His was a separate life, in which he must discover new work and new pleasures for himself. He fought his tears for a while, then, quite overcome, turned and sobbed bitterly in his godmother's arms.

She comforted him and then she whispered to him, in her sweet, strong, cheerful voice, "Never mind!"

"No, I don't think I do mind. That is, I *won't* mind," he replied, catching the courage of her tone and speaking like a man, though he was still such a mere boy.

"That is right, my prince! That is being like a prince. Now that we know exactly where we are let us put our shoulders to the wheel and then——"

"We are in Hopeless Tower and there is no wheel to put our shoulders to," said the child sadly.

"You little matter-of-fact goose! It is well for you that you have a godmother called——"

"What?" he eagerly asked.

"Stuff-and-nonsense."

"Stuff-and-nonsense! What a funny name!"

"Some people give it me, but they are not my most intimate friends. These call me—never mind what," added the old woman, with a soft twinkle in her eyes. "So as you know me, and know me well, you may give me any name you please. It doesn't matter. But I am your godmother, child. I have few godchildren. Those I have love me dearly and find me the greatest blessing in all the world."

"I can well believe it," cried the little lame prince, and forgot his troubles as he looked at her—as her figure dilated, her eyes grew lustrous as stars, her very clothing brightened, and the whole room seemed filled with her beautiful and beneficent presence like light.

He could have looked at her forever, half in love, half in awe, but suddenly she dwindled down into the little old woman all in gray and, with a malicious twinkle in her eyes, asked for the traveling cloak.

"Bring it out of the rubbish cupboard, and shake the dust off it, quick!" she said to Prince Dolor, who hung his head, rather ashamed. "Spread it out on the floor, and wait until the split closes and the edges turn up like a rim all round. Then go and open the skylight. Mind, I say *open the skylight.* Set yourself down in the middle of it, like a frog on a water-lily leaf. Say 'Abracadabra, dum dum dum,' and see what will happen!"

The prince burst into a fit of laughing. It all seemed so exceedingly silly. He wondered that a wise old woman like his godmother should talk such nonsense.

"Stuff-and-nonsense, you mean," said she, answering, to his great alarm, his unspoken thoughts. "Did I not tell you some people called me by that name? Never mind, it doesn't harm me."

And she laughed her merry laugh, as childlike as if she were the prince's age instead of her own, whatever that might be. She certainly was a most extraordinary old woman.

"Believe me or not, it doesn't matter," said she. "Here is the cloak. When you want to go traveling on it, say 'Abracadabra, dum dum dum.' When you want to come back again, say 'Abracadabra, tum tum ti.' That's all. Good-bye."

A puff of pleasant air passing by him, making him feel for the moment quite strong and well, was all the prince was conscious of. His most extraordinary godmother was gone.

"Really now, how rosy Your Royal Highness's cheeks have grown! You seem to have got well already," said the nurse, entering the room.

"I think I have," replied the prince very gently. He felt kind and gentle even to his grim nurse. "And now let me have my dinner, and you go to your sewing as usual."

The instant she was gone, however, taking with her the plates and dishes, which for the first time since his illness he had satisfactorily cleared, Prince Dolor sprang down from his sofa, and with one or two of his froglike jumps, not graceful but convenient, he reached the cupboard where he kept his toys, and looked everywhere for his traveling cloak.

Alas! it was not there.

While he was ill with the doldrums, his nurse, thinking it a good opportunity for putting things to rights, had made a grand clearance of all his "rubbish," as she considered it—his beloved headless horses, broken carts, sheep without feet, and birds without wings—all the treasures of his baby days, which he could not bear to part with. Though he seldom played with them now, he liked just to feel they were there.

They were all gone and with them the traveling cloak. He sat down on the floor, looking at the empty shelves, so beautifully clean and tidy, then burst out sobbing as if his heart would break. But he cried quietly, always quietly. He never let his nurse hear him cry. She only laughed at him, as he felt she would laugh now.

"And it is all my own fault," he cried. "I ought to have taken better care of my godmother's gift. Oh, Godmother, forgive me! I'll never be so careless again. I don't know what the cloak is exactly, but I am sure it is something precious. Help me to find it again. Oh, don't let it be stolen from me. Don't, please!"

"Ha, ha, ha!" laughed a silvery voice. "Why, that traveling cloak is the one thing in the world that nobody can steal. It is of no use to anybody except the owner. Open your eyes, my prince, and see what you shall see."

His dear old godmother, he thought, had turned eagerly around and returned. But no. He only beheld, lying in a corner of the room, all dust and cobwebs, his precious traveling cloak.

Prince Dolor darted toward it, on the way tumbling several times, as he often did tumble, and picked himself up again, never complaining. Snatching it to his breast, he hugged and kissed it, cobwebs and all, as if it had been something alive. Then he began unrolling it, wondering each minute what would happen.

Chapter Five

When Prince Dolor had patiently untied all the knots, a remarkable thing happened. The cloak began to undo itself. Slowly unfolding, it laid itself down on the carpet, as flat as if it had been ironed. The split joined with a little sharp crick-crack, and the rim turned up all around until it was breast-high. For the cloak had grown and grown, and become quite large enough for one person to sit in it, as comfortable as if in a boat.

Rather anxiously, the prince watched the cloak change shape and size. It was such an extraordinary, not to say a frightening, thing. However, he was no coward, but a boy, who, if he had been like other boys, would doubtless have grown up daring and adventurous—a soldier, a sailor, or the like. As it was, he could only show his courage by being afraid of nothing, and by doing boldly all that it was in his narrow powers to do.

He said to himself, "What a goose I am! As if my dear godmother would ever have given me anything to hurt me. Here goes!"

So, with one of his active leaps, he sprang right into the middle of the cloak, where he squatted down, wrapping his arms tight around his knees, for they shook a little and his heart beat fast. But there he sat, steady and silent, waiting for what might happen next.

Nothing did happen. He began to think nothing would, and to feel rather disappointed, when he recollected the words he had been told to repeat—"Abracadabra, dum, dum, dum!"

He repeated them, laughing all the while, they seemed such nonsense. And then—and then the cloak rose, slowly and steadily, at first only a few inches, then gradually higher and higher, till it nearly touched the skylight. Prince Dolor's head actually bumped against the glass, or would have done so, had he not crouched down, crying, "Oh, please don't hurt me!" in a most melancholy voice.

Then he suddenly remembered his godmother's express command—"Open the skylight!"

Regaining his courage at once, without a moment's delay, he lifted his head and began searching for the bolt, the cloak meanwhile remaining perfectly still, balanced in air. But the minute the window was opened, out it sailed, right out into the fresh air, with nothing between it and the cloudless blue.

Prince Dolor had never felt any such delicious sensation before!

How happy the little prince was when he got out of Hopeless Tower, and found himself for the first time in the pure open air, with the sky above him and the earth below.

True, there was nothing but earth and sky. There were no houses, no trees, no rivers, mountains, seas—not a beast on the ground, or a bird in the air. But to him even the level plain looked beautiful. And then there was the glorious arch of the sky, with a little young moon sitting in the west like a baby queen. And the evening breeze was so sweet and fresh, it kissed him like his godmother's kisses. And by and by a few stars came out, first two or three, and then quantities—quantities! So that, when he began to count them, he was utterly bewildered.

By this time, however, the cool breeze had become cold, the mist gathered, and as he had no outdoor clothes, poor Prince Dolor was not very comfortable. The dews fell damp on his curls. He began to shiver.

Perhaps I had better go home, he thought.

But how? For in his excitement the other words that his godmother

had told him to use had slipped his memory. They were only a little different from the first, but in that slight difference all the importance lay. As he repeated his "Abracadabra," trying ever so many other syllables after it, the cloak only went faster and faster, skimming on through the dusky, empty air.

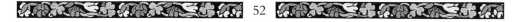

The poor little prince began to feel frightened. What if his wonderful traveling cloak should keep on thus traveling, perhaps to the world's end, carrying with it a poor, tired, hungry boy, who, after all, was beginning to think there was something very pleasant in supper and bed?

"Dear Godmother," he cried pitifully, "do help me! Tell me just this once and I'll never forget again."

Instantly the words came rushing into his head—"Abracadabra, tum, tum, ti!" Was that it? Ah, yes! For the cloak began to turn slowly. He repeated the charm again, more distinctly and firmly, when it gave a gentle dip, like like a nod of satisfaction, and immediately started back, as fast as ever, in the direction of the tower.

He reached the skylight, which he found exactly as he had left it, and slipped in, cloak and all, as easily as he had got out. He had scarcely reached the floor, and was still sitting in the middle of his traveling cloak—like a frog on a water-lily leaf, as his godmother had described it—when he heard his nurse's voice outside.

"Bless us! what has become of Your Royal Highness all this time? To sit stupidly here at the window till it is quite dark, and leave the skylight open, too. Prince! What can you be thinking of? You are the silliest boy I ever knew."

"Am I?" he said absently, never heeding her crossness, for his only anxiety was lest she might find out anything.

She would have been a very clever person to have done so. The instant Prince Dolor got off it, the cloak folded itself up into the tiniest possible parcel, tied all its own knots, and rolled itself of its own accord into the farthest and darkest corner of the room. If the nurse had seen it, which she didn't, she would have taken it for a mere bundle of rubbish not worth noticing.

Shutting the skylight with an angry bang, she brought in the supper and lit the candles, her usual unhappy expression on her face. But Prince Dolor hardly saw it. He only saw, hidden in the corner where nobody else would see it, his wonderful traveling cloak. And though his supper

was not particularly nice, he ate it heartily, scarcely hearing a word of his nurse's grumbling, which tonight seemed to have taken the place of her sullen silence.

Poor woman! he thought, when he paused a minute to listen and look at her, with those quiet, happy eyes, so like his mother's. Poor woman! *She* hasn't got a traveling cloak!

And when he was left alone at last, and crept into his little bed, where he lay awake a good while, watching what he called his "sky garden," all planted with stars, like flowers, his main thought was, I must be up very early tomorrow morning and get my lessons done, and then I'll go traveling all over the world on my beautiful cloak.

So, next day he opened his eyes with the sun, and went with a good heart to his lessons. They had hitherto been the main amusement of his dull life. Now, he found them a little dull. But he tried to be good and when his mind went wandering after the dark dusty corner where lay his precious treasure, he resolutely called it back again.

"For," he said, "how ashamed my godmother would be of me if I grew up a stupid boy."

But the instant lessons were done, and he was alone in the empty room, he crept across the floor, undid the shabby little bundle, his fingers trembling with eagerness. He climbed on the chair, and from there to the table, so as to unbar the skylight—he forgot nothing now—said his magic charm, and was away out of the window, as children say, "in a few minutes less than no time!"

Nobody missed him. He was accustomed to sit so quietly always, that his nurse, though only in the next room, perceived no difference. And besides, she might have gone in and out a dozen times, and it would have been just the same. She never could have discovered his absence.

For the clever godmother took a quantity of moonshine, or some equally convenient material, and made an image, which she set on the windowsill reading, or by the table drawing, where it looked so like Prince Dolor that any common observer would never have guessed the deception. Even the boy would have been puzzled to know which was the image and which was himself.

And all this while the happy little fellow was away, floating in the air on his magic cloak, and seeing all sorts of wonderful things—or they seemed wonderful to him, who had up to then seen nothing at all.

First, there were the flowers that grew on the plain, which, whenever the cloak came near enough, he strained his eyes to look at. They were very tiny, but very beautiful—white saxifrage, and yellow lotus, and ground thistles, purple and bright, with many others the names of which Prince Dolor did not know, although he tried to find them out by recalling any pictures he had seen of them. But he was too far off, and although it was pleasant enough to admire them as brilliant patches of color, still he would have liked to examine them all. He was a very *examining* boy.

I wonder, he thought, whether I could see better through a pair of glasses like those my nurse reads with, and takes such care of. How I would take care of them, too, if only I had a pair!

Immediately, he felt something queer and hard fixing itself onto the bridge of his nose. It was a pair of the prettiest gold spectacles ever seen. And looking downwards, he found that, though ever so high above the ground, he could see every minute blade of grass, every tiny bud and flower—even the insects that walked over them.

"Thank you, thank you!" he cried in a gush of gratitude to anybody or everybody, but especially to his dear godmother, whom he felt sure had given him this new present. He amused himself with it for ever so long, with his chin pressed on the rim of the cloak, gazing down upon the grass, every square foot of which was a mine of wonders.

Then, just to rest his eyes, he turned them up to the sky, the blue, bright, empty sky, which he had looked at so often and seen nothing.

Now, surely there was something. A long, black, wavy line, moving on in the distance, not by chance, as the clouds move apparently, but deliberately, as if it were alive. He might have seen it before, he almost thought he had, but then he could not tell what it was. Looking at it through his spectacles, he discovered that it really was alive. It was a long string of birds, flying one after the other, their wings moving steadily and their heads pointed in one direction, as steadily as if each were a little ship, guided invisibly by an unerring helm.

"They must be the passage birds flying seaward!" cried the boy, who had read a little about them, and had a great talent for putting two and two together and finding out all he could. "Oh, how I should like to see them quite close, and to know where they come from, and where they are going! How I wish I knew everything in all the world!"

A silly speech for even an examining little boy to make; because, as

we grow older, the more we know, the more we find out there is to know. And Prince Dolor blushed when he had said it, and hoped nobody had heard him.

Apparently somebody had, however, for the cloak gave a sudden bound forward, and presently he found himself high up in the air, in the very middle of that band of ærial travelers, who had no magic cloak to travel on, nothing except their wings. Yet there they were, making their fearless way through the sky.

Prince Dolor looked at them, as one after the other they glided past him. And they looked at him—those pretty swallows, with their changing necks and bright eyes—as if wondering to meet in midair such an extraordinary kind of bird.

"Oh, I wish I were going with you, you lovely creatures!" cried the boy. "I'm getting so tired of this dull plain, and the dreary and lonely tower. I do so want to see the world! Pretty swallows, dear swallows! tell me what it looks like—the beautiful, wonderful world!"

But the swallows flew past him—steadily, slowly, pursuing their course as if inside each little head had been a mariner's compass, to guide them safe over land and sea, direct to the place where they desired to go.

The boy looked after them with envy. For a long time he followed with his eyes the faint wavy black line as it floated away, sometimes changing its curves a little, but never deviating from its settled course, until it vanished entirely out of sight.

Then he settled himself down in the center of the cloak, feeling quite sad and lonely.

"I think I'll go home," said he, and repeated his "Abracadabra, tum, tum, ti!" with a rather heavy heart. The more he had, the more he wanted.

He did not wish to vex his godmother by calling for her, and telling her how unhappy he was, in spite of all her goodness. He just kept his trouble to himself, went back to his lonely tower, and spent three days in silent melancholy without even attempting another journey on his traveling cloak.

Chapter Six

The fourth day it happened that the deaf man paid his accustomed visit, after which Prince Dolor's spirits rose. They always did, when he got the new books, which, just to relieve his conscience, the king of Nomansland regularly sent to his nephew with many new toys, too, although they were disregarded now.

"Toys indeed! When I'm a big boy," said the prince with disdain, and would scarcely condescend to mount a rockinghorse, which had come, somehow or other, packed on the back of the other, the great black horse, which stood and fed contentedly at the bottom of the tower.

Prince Dolor leaned over and looked at it, and thought how grand it must be to get upon its back—this grand live steed—and ride away, like the pictures of knights.

"Suppose I was a knight," he said to himself, "then I should be obliged to ride out and see the world."

But he kept all these thoughts to himself, and just sat still, devouring his new books until he had come to the end of them all.

I wonder, he thought, I wonder what it feels like to be on the back of a horse, galloping away, or holding the reins in a carriage, and tearing across the country, or jumping a ditch, or running a race, such as I read of or see in pictures. What a lot of things there are that I should like to do! But first, I should like to go and see the world. I'll try.

Apparently it was his godmother's plan always to let him try, and try hard, before he gained anything. This day the knots that tied up his traveling cloak were more than usually troublesome, and it was a full half hour before he got out into the open air and found himself floating merrily over the top of the tower.

Up to now, in all his journeys he had never let himself go out of sight of home, for the dreary building, after all, was home—he remembered no other. But now he felt sick of the very look of his tower, with its round smooth walls and level battlements.

"Off we go!" cried he, when the cloak stirred itself with a slight slow motion, as if awaiting his orders. "Anywhere—anywhere, so that I am away from here, and out into the world."

As he spoke, the cloak, as if seized suddenly with a new idea, bounded forward and went skimming through the air, faster than the very fastest railway train.

"Gee-up, gee-up!" cried Prince Dolor in great excitement. "This is as good as riding a race."

And he patted the cloak as if it had been a horse—that is, in the way he supposed horses ought to be patted. And he tossed his head back to meet the fresh breeze, and pulled his collar up, as he felt the wind grow keener and colder, colder than anything he had ever known.

"What does it matter though?" said he. "I'm a boy, and boys ought not to mind anything."

Still, for all his good will, by and by, he began to shiver exceedingly. Also, he had come away without his dinner, and he grew frightfully hungry. And to add to everything, the sunshiny day changed into rain, and being high up, in the very midst of the clouds, he got soaked through and through in a very few minutes.

"Shall I turn back?" he wondered. "Suppose I say 'Abracadabra'?"

Here he stopped, for already the cloak gave an obedient lurch, as if it were expecting to be sent home immediately.

"No—I can't—I can't go back! I must go forward and see the world.

But oh! If I had but the shabbiest old rug to shelter one from the rain, or the driest morsel of bread and cheese, just to keep me from starving! Still, I don't mind much. I'm a prince, and ought to be able to stand anything. Hold on, cloak, we'll make the best of it."

It was a most curious circumstance, but no sooner had he said this than he felt stealing over his knees something warm and soft. It was a most beautiful bearskin, which folded itself round him quite naturally, and cuddled him up as closely as if he had been the cub of the kind old mother bear that once owned it. Then feeling in his pocket, which suddenly stuck out in a marvelous way, he found, not exactly bread and cheese, nor even sandwiches, but a packet of the most delicious food he had ever tasted. It was not meat, nor pudding, but a combination of both, and it served him excellently for both. He ate his dinner with the greatest gusto imaginable, until he grew so thirsty he did not know what to do.

"Couldn't I have just one drop of water, if it didn't trouble you too much, kindest of godmothers."

For he really thought this want was beyond her power to supply. All the water that supplied Hopeless Tower was pumped up with difficulty, from a deep artesian well—there were such things known in Nomansland—which had been dug at the foot of it. But around, for miles upon miles, the desolate plain was perfectly dry. And above it, high in the air, how could he expect to find a well, or to get even a drop of water?

He forgot one thing—the rain. While he spoke, it came on in another wild burst, as if the clouds had poured themselves out in a passion of crying, wetting him certainly, but leaving behind, in a large glass vessel that he had never noticed before, enough water to quench the thirst of at least two or three boys. And it was so fresh, so pure—as water from the clouds always is, when it does not catch the soot from city chimneys and other defilements—that he drank it, every drop, with the greatest delight and content.

Also, as soon as it was empty, the rain filled it again, so that he was able to wash his face and hands and refresh himself. Then the sun came

out and dried him in no time. After that he curled himself up under the bearskin rug, and though he determined to be the most wide-awake boy imaginable, being so exceedingly snug and warm and comfortable, Prince Dolor condescended to shut his eyes, just for one minute. The next minute he was sound asleep.

When he awoke, he found himself floating over a country quite unlike anything he had ever seen before.

Yet it was nothing but what most children see every day and never notice—a pretty country landscape. It had no particular features—nothing in it grand or lovely; it was simply pretty, nothing more. Yet to Prince Dolor, who had never gone beyond his lonely tower and level plain, it appeared the most charming sight imaginable.

First, there was a river. It came tumbling down the hillside, frothing and foaming, playing hide and seek among rocks, then bursting out in noisy fun like a child, to bury itself in deep, still pools. Afterward it went steadily on for a while, like a good grownup person, till it came to another big rock, where it misbehaved itself extremely. It turned into a cataract and went tumbling over and over, after a fashion that made the prince—who had never seen water before, except in his bath or his drinking cup—clap his hands with delight.

"It is so active, so alive! I like things active and alive!" he cried, and watched it shimmering and dancing, whirling and leaping, till, after a few windings and vagaries, it settled into a respectable stream. After that it went along, deep and quiet, but flowing steadily on, until it reached a large lake, into which it slipped, and so ended its course.

All this the boy saw, either with his own naked eye, or through his gold spectacles. He saw also as in a picture, beautiful but silent, many other things, which struck him with wonder, especially a grove of trees.

Only think, to have lived to his age (which he himself did not know, as he did not know his own birthday) and never to have seen trees! As he floated over these oaks, they seemed to him—trunks, branches, and leaves—the most curious sight imaginable.

"If I could only get nearer, so as to touch them," he said, and immediately the obedient cloak ducked down. Prince Dolor snatched at the topmost twig of the tallest tree, and caught a bunch of leaves in his hand. He examined his leaves with the greatest curiosity—and also a little caterpillar that he found walking over one of them. He coaxed it to take an additional walk over his finger, which it did with the greatest dignity and decorum, as if it, Mr. Caterpillar, were the most important individual in existence. It amused him for a long time; and when a sudden gust of wind blew it overboard, leaves and all, he felt quite disconsolate.

"Still, there must be many live creatures in the world besides caterpillars. I should like to see a few of them."

The cloak gave a little dip down, as if to say "All right, my prince,"

and bore him across the oak forest to a long fertile valley. It was made up of cornfields, pasturefields, lanes, hedges, brooks, and ponds. Also, in it were what the prince had desired to see, a quantity of living creatures, wild and tame. Cows and horses, lambs and sheep, fed in the meadows. Pigs and fowls walked about the farmyards, and, in lonelier places, hares scurried, rabbits burrowed, and pheasants and partridges, with many other smaller birds, inhabited the fields and woods.

Through his wonderful spectacles the prince could see everything, but it was a silent picture. He was too high up to catch anything except a faint murmur, which only aroused his desire to hear more.

"I have as good as two pairs of eyes," he said to himself. "I wonder if my godmother would give me a second pair of ears."

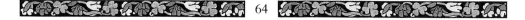

Scarcely had he spoken, than he found lying on his lap the most curious little parcel, all done up in silvery paper. And it contained a pair of silver ears, which, when he tried them on, fitted so exactly over his own that he hardly felt them, except for the difference they made in his hearing.

Prince Dolor, who had lived all his days in the dead silence of Hopeless Tower, heard for the first time the sounds of the visible world. He heard winds blowing, water flowing, trees stirring, insects whirring, the various cries of birds and beasts—lowing cattle, bleating sheep, grunting pigs, and cackling hens—all the infinite discords that somehow make a beautiful harmony.

He listened, listened, as if he could never hear enough. And he looked and looked, as if he could not gaze enough. Above all, the motion of the animals delighted him—cows walking, horses galloping, little lambs and calves running races across the meadows were such a treat for him to watch—he who was always so quiet. But, these creatures having four legs, and he only two, the difference did not strike him painfully.

Still, by and by, he began to want something more than he had, something that would be quite fresh and new.

"Godmother," he said, having now begun to believe that, whether he saw her or not, he could always speak to her with full confidence that she would hear him—"Godmother, all these creatures I like exceedingly, but I should like better to see a creature like myself. Couldn't you show me just one little boy?"

There was a sigh behind him—it might have been only the wind—and the cloak remained so long balanced motionless in air, that he was half afraid his godmother had forgotten him, or was offended with him for asking too much. Suddenly, a shrill whistle startled him, even through his silver ears, and looking downward, he saw start up, from behind a bush on a common, something . . .

It was neither a sheep, nor a horse, nor a cow—nothing upon four legs. This creature had only two, but they were long, straight, and strong. And it had a lithe, active body, and a curly head of black hair set upon its shoulders. It was a boy, a shepherd boy, about the prince's own age, but, oh! so different.

Not that he was an ugly boy, although his face was almost as red as his hands, and his shaggy hair was matted like the backs of his own sheep. He was rather a nice-looking lad and seemed so bright, and healthy, and good-tempered that the little prince watched him with great admiration.

"Might he come and play with me? I would drop down to the ground to him, or fetch him up to me here. Oh, how nice it would be if only I had a little boy to play with me!" he said to himself.

But the cloak, usually so obedient to his wishes, disobeyed him now. There were evidently some things that his godmother either could not or would not give. The cloak hung stationary, high in the air, never attempting to descend. The shepherd lad evidently took it for a large bird and, shading his eyes, looked up at it, making the prince's heart beat fast. But then the boy turned around, with a long, loud whistle.

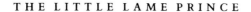

Stretching, for he had been evidently half asleep, he began flopping his shoulders with his arms, to wake and warm himself. His dog, a rough collie, who had been guarding the sheep meanwhile, began to jump upon him, barking with delight.

"Down, Snap, down! Stop that, or I'll thrash you," the prince heard him say, though with such a rough, hard voice and

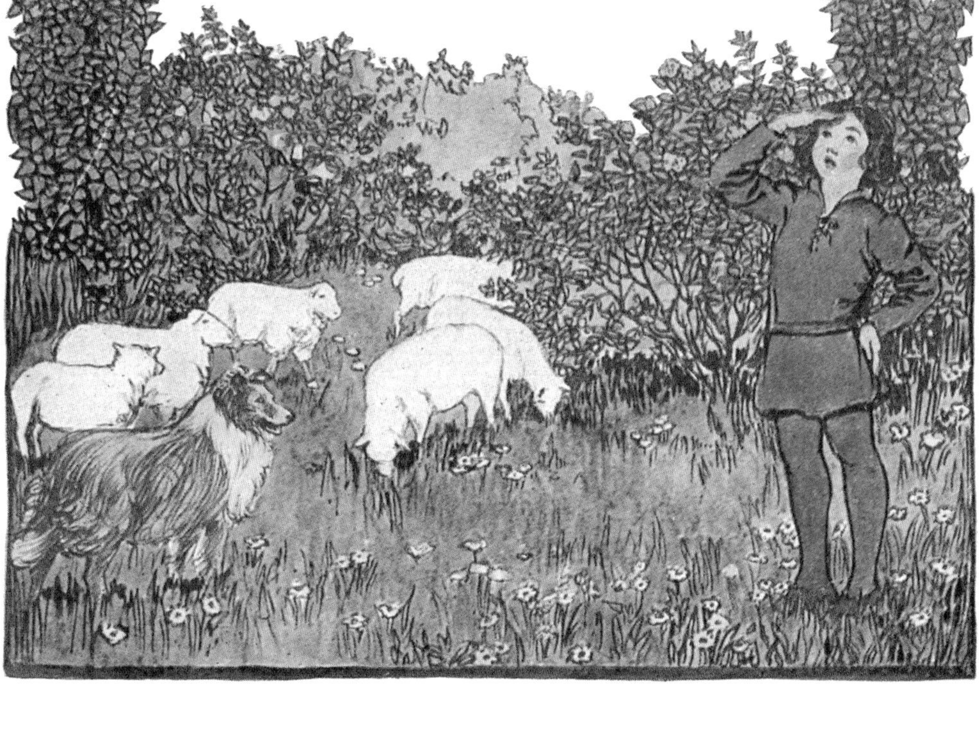

queer pronunciation that it was difficult to make the words out. "Let's warm ourselves by having a race."

They started off together, boy and dog, barking and shouting, until it was doubtful which made the most noise or ran the fastest. A regular steeplechase it was: first across the level common, greatly disturbing the quiet sheep; and then tearing away across country, scrambling through hedges, and leaping ditches, and tumbling up and down over plowed fields. They did not seem to have anything to run for, but it was as if they did it, both of them, for the mere pleasure of motion.

And what a pleasure that seemed! To the dog of course, but scarcely less so to the boy. How he skimmed along over the ground, his cheeks glowing, and his hair flying, and his legs. Oh, what a pair of legs he had!

Prince Dolor watched him with great intentness, and in a state of excitement almost equal to that of the runner himself—for a while. Then the sweet pale face grew a trifle paler, the lips began to quiver and the eyes to fill. "How nice it must be to run like that!" he said softly, thinking that never would he be able to do the same.

Now he understood what his godmother had meant when she gave him his traveling cloak, and why he had heard that sigh—he was sure it was hers—when he had asked to see "just one little boy."

"I think I had rather not look at him again," said the poor little prince, drawing himself back into the center of his cloak, and resuming his favorite posture, with his arms wrapped around his feeble, useless legs.

"You're no good to me," he said, patting them mournfully. "You never will be any good to me. I wonder why I had you at all. I wonder why I was born at all, since I was not to grow up like other little boys. *Why* not?"

Prince Dolor sat a good while thus, or it appeared to him a good while, so many thoughts came and went through his young mind—thoughts of great bitterness, which, little though he was, seemed to make him grow years older in a few minutes.

Then he fancied that the cloak began to rock gently to and fro, with a soothing kind of motion, as if he were in the arms of somebody who did not speak, but loved him and comforted him without need of words; not by deceiving him with false encouragement or hope, but by making him see the plain hard truth, in all its hardness, and thus letting him quietly face it, till it grew softened down, and did not seem nearly so dreadful after all.

Through the dreary silence and blankness, for he had placed himself so that he could see nothing but the sky, and had taken off his silver ears, as well as his gold spectacles—what was the use of either when he had no legs to walk or run?—up from below there rose a delicious sound.

It was just the song of a skylark, mounting higher and higher from the ground, till it came so close that Prince Dolor could distinguish its quivering wings and tiny body, almost too tiny to contain such a gush of music.

"O, you beautiful, beautiful bird!" he cried, "I should dearly like to take you in and cuddle you. That is, if I could—if I dared."

But he hesitated. The little brown creature with its loud heavenly voice almost made him afraid. Nevertheless, it also made him happy. And he watched and listened, so absorbed that he forgot all regret and pain, forgot everything in the world except the little lark.

It soared and soared, and he was just wondering if it would soar out of sight, and what in the world he should do when it was gone, when it suddenly closed its wings, as larks do, when they mean to drop to the ground. But, instead of dropping to the ground, it dropped right into the little boy's collar.

What felicity! If it would only stay! A tiny soft thing to fondle and kiss, to sing to him all day long, and be his playfellow and companion, tame and tender, while to the rest of the world it was a wild bird of the air. What a pride, what a delight! To have somebody that nobody else had, something all his own. As the traveling cloak traveled on, he little heeded where, and the lark still stayed, nestled against him, hopped from his hand to his shoulder, and kissed him with its dainty beak, as if it loved him, Prince Dolor forgot his grief, and was entirely happy.

But when he got in sight of Hopeless Tower, a painful thought struck him. "My pretty bird, what am I to do with you? If I take you into my room and shut you up there, you, a wild skylark of the air, what will become of you? I am used to this, but you are not. You will be so miserable. And suppose my nurse should find you? She can't bear the sound of singing. Besides, I remember her once telling me that the nicest thing she ever ate in her life was lark pie!"

The little boy shivered all over at the thought. And, though the merry lark immediately broke into the loudest carol, as if saying derisively that he defined anybody to eat *him*, Prince Dolor was still very uneasy. In another minute he had made up his mind.

"No, my bird, nothing so dreadful shall happen to you if I can help it. I would rather do without you altogether. Yes, I'll try. Fly away, my darling, my beautiful! Good-bye, my merry, merry bird."

Opening his two caressing hands, in which, as if for protection, he had folded it, he let the lark go. It lingered a minute, perching on the rim of the cloak, and looking at him with eyes of almost human tenderness. Then away it flew, far up into the blue sky. It was only a bird.

But, some time after, when Prince Dolor had eaten his supper—somewhat drearily, except for the thought that he could not possibly sup off lark pie now—and gone quietly to bed, the old familiar little bed, where he was accustomed to sleep, or lie awake contentedly thinking—suddenly he heard outside the window a little faint carol—faint but cheerful—cheerful, even though it was the middle of the night.

The dear little lark! it had not flown away after all. And it was truly the most extraordinary bird, for, unlike ordinary larks, it kept hovering about the tower in the silence and darkness of the night, outside the window or over the roof. Whenever he listened for a moment, he heard it singing still.

He went to sleep as happy as a king.

Chapter Seven

"Happy as a king." How far kings are happy Prince Dolor couldn't say, although he had once been a king himself. But he remembered nothing about it, and there was nobody to tell him, except his nurse, who had been forbidden upon pain of death to let him know anything about his dead parents, or the king his uncle, or, indeed, any part of his own history.

Sometimes he speculated about himself, whether he had had a father and mother as other little boys had, what they had been like, and why he had never seen them. But, knowing nothing about them, he did not miss them. Only once or twice, reading pretty stories about little children and their mothers, who helped them when they were in difficulty, and comforted them when they were sick, he, feeling ill and dull and lonely, wondered what had become of his mother, and why she never came to see him.

Then, in his history lessons, of course, he read about kings and princes, and the governments of different countries, and the events that happened there. And though he but faintly took in all this, still he did take it in, a little, and worried about it, and perplexed his nurse with questions, to which she returned sharp and mysterious answers, which only set him thinking the more.

He had plenty of time for thinking. After his last journey in the traveling cloak, the journey that had given him so much pain, his desire to see the world had somehow faded away. He contented himself with reading his books, and looking out of the tower windows, and listening to his beloved little lark, which had come home with him that day, and never left him again.

True, it kept out of the way. And though his nurse sometimes dimly heard it, and said, "What is that horrid noise outside?" she never got the faintest chance of making it into a lark pie. Prince Dolor had his pet all to himself, and though he seldom saw it, he knew it was near him, and he caught continually, at odd hours of the day, and even in the night, fragments of its delicious song.

All during the winter—so far as there ever was any difference between summer and winter in Hopeless Tower—the little bird cheered and amused him. He scarcely needed anything more, not even his traveling cloak, which lay bundled up unnoticed in a corner, tied up in its innumerable knots. Nor did his godmother come near him. It seemed as if she had given these treasures and left him alone, to use them, or lose them, apply them, or misapply them, according to his own choice.

Prince Dolor was now quite a big boy. Not tall. Alas! He never could be tall, with his poor little shrunken legs, which were of no use, only an encumbrance. But he was large and strong, with great sturdy shoulders, and muscular arms, upon which he could swing himself about almost like a monkey. As if in compensation for his useless lower limbs, nature had given extra strength and activity to his arms. His face, too, was very handsome. It was thinner, firmer, and more manly, but still the sweet face of his childhood—his mother's own face.

The boy was very smart, too. He could learn almost anything he chose. He never gave up his lessons until he had learned them all. He never thought it a punishment that he had to work at them.

But, he thought, men work, and it must be so grand to be a man; a prince too. I fancy princes work harder than anybody, except kings. The princes I read about generally turn into kings. "Nurse"—one day he startled her with a sudden question—"tell me, shall I ever be a king?"

The woman stood, perplexed beyond expression. So long a time had passed by since her crime—if it was a crime—and her sentence, that she now seldom thought of either. Even her punishment—to be shut up for life in Hopeless Tower—she had gradually got used to. Used also to the little lame prince, her charge, whom at first she had hated, though she carefully did everything to keep him alive, since upon him her own life hung. But she had ceased to hate him, and, in a sort of way, almost loved him, at least enough to be sorry for him—an innocent child, imprisoned here until he grew into an old man and became a dull, worn-out creature like herself. Sometimes, watching him, she felt more sorry for him than even for herself. And then, seeing she looked a less miserable and ugly woman, he did not shrink from her as usual.

He did not now. "Nurse—dear nurse," he said, "I don't mean to vex you, but tell me—what is a king? Shall I ever be one?"

When she began to think less of herself and more of her child, the woman's courage increased. The idea came to her—what harm would it be, even if he did know his own history? Perhaps he ought to know it, for there had been various ups and downs, usurpations, revolutions, and restorations in Nomansland, as in most other countries. Something might happen. Who could tell? Changes might occur. Possibly a crown would even yet be set upon those pretty, fair curls, which she began to think prettier than ever when she saw the imaginary coronet upon them.

She sat down, considering whether her oath, never to "say a word" to Prince Dolor about himself, would be broken if she were to take a pencil and write what was to be told. A mere quibble—a mean, miserable quibble. But then she was a miserable woman, more to be pitied than scorned.

After long doubt, and with great trepidation, she put her finger to her lips, and taking the prince's slate—with the sponge tied to it, ready to rub out the writing in a minute—she wrote, "You are a king."

Prince Dolor started. His face grew pale, and then flushed all over. His eyes glistened. He held himself erect. Lame as he was, anybody could see he was born to be a king.

"Hush!" said his nurse, as he was beginning to speak. And then, terribly frightened all the while, she wrote down in a few hurried sentences his history. How his parents had died and his uncle had usurped his throne and sent him to end his days in this lonely tower.

"I, too," she added, bursting into tears. "Unless, indeed, you could get out into the world, and fight for your rights like a man. And fight for me too, my prince, that I may not die in this desolate place."

"Poor old nurse!" said the boy compassionately. For somehow, boy as he was, when he heard he was born to be a king, he felt like a man—like a king—who could afford to be tender because he was strong.

He scarcely slept that night, and even though he heard his little lark singing in the sunrise, he barely listened to it. Things more serious and important had taken possession of his mind.

Suppose, he thought, I were to do as she says, and go out into the world, no matter how it hurts me—the world of people, active people, as active as that boy I saw. They might only laugh at me, poor helpless creature that I am. But still I might show them I could do something. At any rate, I might go and see if there was anything for me to do. "Godmother, help me!"

It was so long since he had asked for her help, that he was hardly surprised when he got no answer, only the little lark outside the window sang louder and louder, and the sun rose, flooding the room with light.

Prince Dolor sprang out of bed, and began dressing himself, which was hard work, for he was not used to it. He had always been accustomed to depend upon his nurse for everything.

But I must now learn to be independent, he thought. Fancy a king being dressed like a baby!

So he did the best he could—awkwardly but cheerily—and then he leaped to the corner where lay his traveling cloak. He untied it as before, and watched it unrolling itself, which it did rapidly, with a hearty goodwill, as if quite tired of idleness. So was Prince Dolor, or he felt as if he was. He jumped into the middle of it, said his charm, and was out through the skylight immediately.

"Good-bye, pretty lark!" he shouted, as he passed it on the wing, still warbling its carol to the newly risen sun. "You have been my pleasure, my delight. Now I must go and work. Sing to old nurse till I come back again. Perhaps she'll hear you, perhaps she won't, but it will do her good all the same. Good-bye!"

But, as the cloak hung irresolute in air, he suddenly remembered that he had not determined where to go. Indeed, he did not know, and there was nobody to tell him.

"Godmother," he cried, in much perplexity, "you know what I want. At least, I hope you do, for I hardly do myself. Take me where I ought to go. Show me, whatever I ought to see. Never mind what I like to see," he said as a sudden idea came into his mind that he might see many painful and disagreeable things. But this journey was not for pleasure as before. He was not a baby now, to do nothing but play. Big boys do not always play. Nor do men—they work. Thus much Prince Dolor knew, though very little more. And as the cloak started off, traveling faster than he had ever known it to do—through skyland and cloud land, over freezing mountaintops, and desolate stretches of forest, and smiling cultivated plains, and great lakes that seemed to him almost as shoreless as the sea—he was often rather frightened. But he crouched down, silent and quiet; what was the use of making a fuss? And, wrapping himself up in his bearskin, he waited for what was to happen.

After some time he heard a murmur in the distance, increasing more and more until it grew like the hum of a gigantic hive of bees. And, stretching his chin over the rim of his cloak, Prince Dolor saw—far, far below him, yet with his gold spectacles and silver ears on, he could distinctly hear and see—a great metropolis. There was its network of streets, its crowds of people, its tall rows of houses, its grand public buildings, churches, and squares. There, too, were its miserable little back alleys, where dirty children played in gutters, where men reeled tipsy and women fought—where even young boys went about picking pockets. And all this wretchedness was close behind the grandeur—like the two sides of the leaf of a book.

Prince Dolor had to be a king—that is, a boy with a kingly nature—to be able to stand such a sight without being utterly overcome. But he was very much bewildered, as bewildered as a blind person who is suddenly made to see.

He gazed down on the city below him, and then put his hand over his eyes. "I can't bear to look at it, it is so beautiful—so dreadful. And I don't understand it—not one bit. There is nobody to tell me about it. I wish I had somebody to speak to."

"Do you? Then pray speak to me. I was always considered good at conversation."

The voice that squeaked out this reply was an excellent imitation of the human one, though it came only from a bird. It was no lark this time, however, but a great black and white creature that flew into the cloak, and began walking round and round on the edge of it with a dignified stride, one foot before the other.

"I haven't the honor of your acquaintance, sir," said the boy politely.

"Ma'am, if you please. I am a mother bird, and my name is Mag, and I shall be happy to tell you everything you want to know. For I know a great deal and I enjoy talking. My family is of great antiquity. We have built in this palace for hundreds—that is to say, dozens—of years. I am intimately acquainted with the king, the queen, and the little princes and princesses—also with the maids of honor, and all the inhabitants of the city. I talk a good deal, but I always talk sense, and I shall dare say I should be exceedingly useful to a poor little ignorant boy like you."

"I am a prince," said the boy gently.

"All right. And I am a magpie. You will find me a most respectable bird."

"I have no doubt of it," was the polite answer, although he thought in his own mind that Mag must have a very good opinion of herself. But she was a lady and a stranger, so, of course, he was civil to her.

She settled herself at his elbow, and began to chatter away, pointing out with one skinny claw while she balanced herself on the other, every object of interest, evidently believing, as no doubt all its inhabitants did, that there was no capital in the world like the great metropolis of Nomansland. Mag said that it was the finest city that ever was built. And of course she knew.

Nevertheless, there were a few things in it that surprised Prince Dolor, and as he had said, he could not understand them at all. One half the people seemed so happy and busy, hurrying up and down the full streets, or driving lazily along the parks in their grand carriages, while the other half were so wretched and miserable.

"Can't the world be made a little more level? I would try to do it if I were the king."

"But you're not the king: only a little goose of a boy," returned the magpie loftily. "And I'm here not to explain things, only to show them. Shall I show you the royal palace?"

It was a very magnificent palace. It had terraces and gardens, battlements and towers. It extended over acres of ground, and had in it rooms enough to accommodate half the city. Its windows looked in all directions, but none of them had any particular view—except a small one, high up toward the roof, which looked onto the Beautiful Mountains. But since the queen died there, it had been closed, indeed boarded up, the magpie said. It was so little and inconvenient, that nobody cared to live in it.

Besides, the lower apartments, which had no view, were magnificent—worthy of being inhabited by His Majesty the King.

"I should like to see the king," said Prince Dolor.

Chapter Eight

"Ah," said the magpie, "no audiences today. The king is ill, though His Majesty does not wish it to be generally known. It would be so very inconvenient. He can't see you, but perhaps you might like to go and take a look at him, in a way I often do? It is so very amusing."

The prince was now too excited to talk much. Was he not going to see the king his uncle, who had succeeded his father, and dethroned himself, had stepped into all the pleasant things that he, Prince Dolor, ought to have had, and shut him up in a desolate tower? What was he like, this great, bad, clever man? Had he got all the things he wanted, which another ought to have had? And did he enjoy them?

"Nobody knows," answered the magpie, just as if she had been sitting inside the prince's heart, instead of on the top of his shoulder. "He is a king, and that's enough. For the rest nobody knows."

As she spoke, Mag flew down onto the palace roof, where the cloak had rested, settling down between the great stacks of chimneys as comfortably as if it was the ground. She pecked at the tiles with her beak—truly she was a wonderful bird—and immediately a little hole opened, a sort of door, through which could be seen distinctly the chamber below.

"Look in quickly, my prince, for I must soon shut it up again."

But the boy hesitated. "Isn't it rude? Won't they, perhaps, think us—intruding?"

"Oh dear no! There's a hole like this in every palace. Dozens of holes, indeed. Everybody knows it, but nobody speaks of it. Intrusion! Why, though the royal family are supposed to live shut up behind stone walls ever so thick, all the world knows that they live in a glass house where everybody can see them, and throw a stone at them. Now, pop down on your knees, and take a peep at His Majesty."

His Majesty!

The prince gazed eagerly down into a large room, the largest room he had ever beheld, with furniture and hangings grander than anything he could have ever imagined. A stray sunbeam, coming through a crevice of the darkened windows, struck across the carpet, and it was the loveliest carpet ever woven, just like a bed of flowers to walk over. But nobody walked over it. The room was perfectly empty and silent.

"Where is the king?" asked the puzzled boy.

"There," said Mag, pointing with one wrinkled claw to a magnificent bed, large enough to contain six people. In the center of it, just visible under the silken counterpane, quite straight and still, with its head on the lace pillow, lay a small figure, something like a wax statue, fast asleep. Very fast asleep! There were many sparkling rings on the tiny yellow hands that were curled a little, helplessly, like a baby's, outside the coverlet. The eyes were shut, the nose looked sharp and thin, and the long gray beard hid the mouth, and lay over the breast. A sight not ugly, nor frightening, only solemn and quiet. And so very silent. Two little flies, buzzing about the curtains of the bed, were the only audible sound.

"Is that the king?" whispered Prince Dolor.

"Yes," replied the bird.

He had been angry—furiously angry—ever since he knew how his uncle had taken the crown, and sent him, a poor little helpless child, to be shut up for life, just as if he had been dead. Many times the boy had felt as if, king as he was, he should like to strike him, this great, strong, wicked man.

Why, you might as well have struck a baby! How helpless he lay with his eyes shut, and his idle hands folded. They had no more work to do, bad or good.

"What is the matter with him?" asked the prince again.

"He is dead," said the magpie with a croak.

No, there was not the least use in being angry with him now. On the contrary, the prince felt almost sorry for him, except that he looked so peaceful, with all his cares at rest. And this was being dead? So, even kings died?

"Well, well, he hadn't an easy life, folks say, for all his grandeur. Perhaps he is glad it is over. Good-bye, Your Majesty."

With another cheerful tap of her beak, Mistress Mag shut down the little door in the tiles, and Prince Dolor's first and last sight of his uncle was ended.

He sat in the center of his traveling cloak silent and thoughtful.

"What shall we do now?" asked the magpie. "There's nothing much more to be done with His Majesty, except a fine funeral, which I shall certainly go and see. All the world will. He interested the world exceedingly when he was alive, and he ought to do it now he's dead—just once more. And since he can't hear me, I may as well say that, on the whole, His Majesty is much better off dead than alive—if we can only get somebody in his place. There'll soon be such a fuss in the city. Suppose we float up again and see it all. At a safe distance, though. It will be such fun."

"What will be fun?"

"A revolution."

As soon as the cathedral bell began to toll, and the minute guns began to fire, announcing to the kingdom that it was without a king, the people gathered in crowds, stopping at street corners to talk together. The murmur now and then rose into a shout, and the shout into a roar. When Prince Dolor, quietly floating in upper air, caught the sound of their different cries, it seemed to him as if the whole city had gone mad.

"Long live the king!" "The king is dead—down with the king!" "Down with the crown, and the king, too!" "Hurrah for the republic!" "Hurrah for no government at all."

Such were the shouts that traveled up to the traveling cloak. And then began—oh, what a scene!

Revolutions have happened, and may happen again, in other countries besides Nomansland, when wicked kings have helped to make their people wicked too, or out of an unrighteous nation have sprung rulers equally bad; or, without either of these causes, when a restless country has fancied any change better than no change at all.

It is difficult to understand how good can come out of absolute evil—the horrible evil that went on this night under Prince Dolor's very eyes—soldiers shooting people down by hundreds in the streets, scaffolds erected, and houses burned to the ground.

Prince Dolor saw it all. Things happened so fast after one another that they quite confused his faculties.

"Oh, let me go home," he cried at last, covering his ears and shutting his eyes; "only let me go home!" Even his lonely tower seemed home, and its dreariness and silence absolute paradise after all this.

"Good-bye, then," said the magpie, flapping her wings. She had been chatting incessantly all day and all night, for it was actually thus long that Prince Dolor had been hovering over the city, neither eating nor sleeping, with all these terrible things happening under his very eyes. "You've had enough, I suppose, of seeing the world?"

"Oh, I have—I have!" cried the prince with a shudder.

"That is, till next time. All right, Your Royal Highness. You don't know me, but I know you. We may meet again sometime."

She looked at him with her clear piercing eyes, sharp enough to see through everything, and it seemed as if they changed from bird's eyes to human eyes, the very eyes of his godmother, whom he had not seen for ever so long. But the minute afterward she became only a bird, and with a screech and a chatter spread her wings and flew away.

Prince Dolor fell into a kind of swoon, of utter misery, bewilderment, and exhaustion, and when he awoke he found himself in his own room—alone and quiet—with the dawn just breaking, and the long rim of yellow light in the horizon glimmering through the windowpanes.

Chapter Nine

When Prince Dolor sat up in bed, trying to remember where he was, where he had been, and what he had seen the day before, he perceived that his room was empty.

Generally, his nurse woke him coming in and "setting things to rights," as she called it. Now, the dust lay thick upon chairs and tables. There was no harsh voice heard to scold him for not getting up immediately—which this boy did not always do. For he so enjoyed lying still, and thinking lazily, about everything or nothing, that, if he had not tried hard against it, he would certainly have become like those celebrated

Two little men
Who lay in their bed till the clock struck ten.

It was striking ten now, and still no nurse was to be seen. He was rather relieved at first, for he felt so tired. Besides, when he stretched out his arm, he found to his dismay that he had gone to bed in his clothes.

Very uncomfortable he felt, of course, and just a little frightened. Especially when he began to call and call again, but nobody answered. Often he used to think how nice it would be to get rid of his nurse and live in this tower all by himself—like a kind of monarch, able to do everything he liked, and leave undone all that he did not want to do. But now that this seemed really to have happened, he did not like it at all.

"Nurse—dear nurse—please come back!" he called out. "Come back, and I will be the best boy in all the land."

And when she did not come back, and nothing but silence answered his lamentable call, he very nearly began to cry.

"This won't do," he said at last, dashing the tears from his eyes. "It's just like a baby, and I'm a big boy. I shall be a man some day. What has happened, I wonder? I'll go and see."

He sprang out of bed and crawled on his knees from room to room. All the four chambers were deserted—not forlorn or untidy, for everything seemed to have been done for his comfort. The breakfast and dinner-things were laid, the food spread in order. He might live "like a prince," as the proverb is, for several days. But the place was entirely forsaken. There was evidently not a creature but himself in the solitary tower.

A great fear came upon the poor boy. Lonely as his life had been, he had never known what it was to be absolutely alone. A kind of despair seized him—no violent anger or terror, but a sort of patient desolation.

What in the world am I to do? he thought, and sat down in the middle of the floor, half inclined to believe that it would be better to give up entirely, lay himself down and die.

This feeling, however, did not last long, for he was young and strong, and by nature a very courageous boy. There came into his head, somehow or other, a proverb that his nurse had taught him—the people of Nomansland were very fond of proverbs:

For every evil under the sun
There is a remedy, or there's none;
If there is one, try to find it—
If there isn't, never mind it.

"I wonder—is there a remedy now, and could I find it?" cried the prince, jumping up and looking out of the window.

No help there. He only saw the broad, bleak, sunshiny plain—that is, at first. But, by and by, in the circle of mud that surrounded the base of the tower, he perceived distinctly the marks of a horse's hooves, and just in the spot where the deaf man was accustomed to tie up his great black charger, while he himself ascended, there lay the remains of a bundle of hay and a feed of corn.

"Yes, that's it. He has come and gone, taking nurse away with him. Poor nurse! how glad she would be to go!"

That was Prince Dolor's first thought. His second was a passionate indignation at her cruelty, at the cruelty of all the world toward him, a poor little helpless boy. Then he determined—forsaken as he was—to try and hold on to the last, and not to die as long as he could possibly help it.

Anyhow, it would be easier to die here than out in the world, among the terrible doings which he had just beheld. From the midst of which, it suddenly struck him, the deaf man had come and had somehow managed to make the nurse understand that the king was dead, and she need have no fear in going back to the capital, where there was a grand revolution, and everything was turned upside down. So, of course she had gone.

I hope she'll enjoy it, miserable woman—if they don't cut off her head too.

And then a kind of remorse smote him for feeling so bitterly toward her. After all the years she had taken care of him—grudgingly, perhaps, and coldly. Still, she had taken care of him, and that even to the last. Indeed, all his four rooms were as tidy as possible, and his meals were laid out, that he might have no more trouble than could be helped.

"Possibly she did not mean to be cruel. I won't judge her," said he. Afterward he was very glad that he had so determined.

For the second time he tried to dress himself, and then to do everything he could for himself—even to sweeping up the hearth and putting on more coals. "It's a funny thing for a prince to have to do," he said laughing. "But my godmother once said princes need never mind doing anything."

And then he thought a little of his godmother. Not of summoning her, or asking her to help him. She had evidently left him to help himself, and he was determined to try his best to do it, being a very proud and independent boy. But he remembered her, tenderly and regretfully, as if even she had been a little hard upon him—poor, forlorn boy that he was! But he seemed to have seen and learned so much within the last few days, that he scarcely felt like a boy, but a man.

After his first despair, he was not merely comfortable, but actually happy in his solitude, doing everything for himself, and enjoying everything by himself—until bedtime. Then, he did not like it at all.

But the prince had to bear it—and he did bear it—like a prince, for fully five days. All that time he got up in the morning and went to bed at night, without having spoken to a creature, or, indeed, having heard a single sound. For even his little lark was silent. And as for his traveling cloak, either he never thought about it, or else it had been spirited away, for he made no use of it, nor attempted to do so.

A very strange existence it was, those five lonely days. He never entirely forgot it. It threw him back upon himself, and into himself.

On the sixth day, Prince Dolor had a strange composure in his look, but he was very grave, and thin, and white. He had nearly come to the end of his provisions. And what was to happen next? Get out of the tower he could not. The ladder of the deaf man used was always carried away again. And if it had not been, how could the poor boy have used it? And even if he slung or flung himself down, and by miraculous chance came alive to the foot of the tower, how could he run away?

Fate had been very hard to him, or so it seemed.

He made up his mind to die. Not that he wished to die. On the contrary, there was a great deal he wished to live to do. But if he must die, he must. Dying did not seem so very dreadful; not even to lie quiet like his uncle, whom he had entirely forgiven now, and neither be miserable nor naughty any more, and escape all those horrible things that he had seen going on outside the palace, in that awful place that was called "the world."

"It's a great deal nicer here," said the poor little prince, and collected all his pretty things around him—his favorite pictures, which he thought he should like to have near him when he died; his books and toys—no, he had ceased to care for toys now. He only liked them because he had done so as a child. And there he sat very calm and patient, like a king in his castle, waiting for the end.

Still, I wish I had done something first, something worth doing, that somebody might remember me by, he thought. Suppose I had grown a man, and had had work to do, and people to care for, and was so useful and busy that they liked me, and perhaps even forgot I was lame. Then, it would have been nice to live, I think.

A tear came into the little fellow's eyes, and he listened intently through the dead silence for some hopeful sound.

Was there one? Was it his little lark, whom he had almost forgotten? No, nothing half so sweet. But it really was something—something that came nearer and nearer, so that there was no mistaking it. It was the sound of a trumpet, one of the great silver trumpets so admired in Nomansland. Not pleasant music, but very bold, grand, and inspiring.

As he listened to it the boy seemed to recall many things that had slipped his memory for years, and to steel himself for whatever might be going to happen.

What had happened was this.

The poor condemned woman had not been such a wicked woman after all. Perhaps her courage was not wholly disinterested but she had done a very heroic thing. As soon as she learned of the death and burial of the king, and of the changes that were taking place in the country, a daring idea came into her head—to set upon the throne of Nomansland its rightful heir. Thereupon she persuaded the deaf man to take her away with him, and they galloped like the wind from city to city, spreading everywhere the news that Prince Dolor's death and burial had been an invention concocted by his wicked uncle, that he was alive and well, and the noblest young prince that ever was born.

It was a bold stroke, but it succeeded. The country, weary, perhaps, of the late king's harsh rule, and yet glad to save itself from the horrors of the last few days, and the still further horrors of no rule at all, and having no particular interest in the other young princes, jumped at the idea of this prince, who was the son of their late good king and the beloved Queen Dolorez.

"Hurrah for Prince Dolor! Let Prince Dolor be our sovereign!" rang from end to end of the kingdom. Everybody tried to remember what a dear baby he once was—how like his mother, who had been so sweet and kind, and his father, the finest looking king that ever reigned. Nobody remembered his lameness. Or, if they did, they passed it over as a matter of no consequence. They were determined to have him reign over them, boy as he was. Perhaps because he was a boy the great nobles thought they should be able to do as they liked with the country.

Accordingly, with a fickleness not confined to the people of Nomansland, no sooner was the late king laid in his grave than they pronounced him to have been a usurper. They turned all his family out of the palace, and left it empty for the reception of the new sovereign, whom they went to fetch with great rejoicing. A select body of lords, gentlemen, and soldiers traveled night and day in solemn procession through the country, until they reached Hopeless Tower.

There they found the prince, sitting calmly on the floor—deadly pale indeed, for he expected a quite different end from this, and was resolved if he had to die, to die courageously, like a prince and a king.

But when they hailed him as prince and king, and explained to him how matters stood, and went down on their knees before him, offering the crown (on a velvet cushion, with four golden tassels, each nearly as big as his head)—small though he was and lame, which lameness the courtiers pretended not to notice—there came such a glow into his face, such a dignity into his demeanor, that he became beautiful, kinglike.

"Yes," he said, "if you desire it, I will be your king. And I will do my best to make my people happy."

Then there arose, from inside and outside the tower, such a shout as never was yet heard across the lonely plain.

Prince Dolor shrank a little from the deafening sound. "How shall I be able to rule all this great people? You forget, my lords, that I am only a little boy still."

"Not so very little," was the respectful answer. "We have searched in the records, and found that Your Royal Highness—Your Majesty, I mean—is precisely fifteen years old."

"Am I?" said Prince Dolor. And his first thought was a thoroughly childish pleasure that he should now have a birthday, with a whole nation to celebrate it. Then he remembered that his childish days were done. He was a monarch now. Even his nurse, to whom, the moment he saw her, he had held out his hand, kissed it reverently, and called him ceremoniously "His Majesty the King."

"A king must be always a king, I suppose," he said half sadly, when, the ceremonies over, he had been left to himself for just ten minutes, to take off his boy's clothes, and be reattired in magnificent robes, before he was conveyed away from his tower to the royal palace.

He could take nothing with him. Indeed, he soon saw that, however politely they spoke, they would not allow him to take anything. If he was to be their king, he must give up his old life forever. So he looked with tender farewell on his old books, old toys, the furniture he knew so well, and the familiar plain in all its levelness, ugly yet pleasant, simply because it was familiar.

"It will be a new life in a new world," he said to himself; "but I'll remember the old things still. And, oh! if before I go, I could but once see my dear old godmother."

While he spoke, he had laid himself down on the bed for a minute or two, rather tired with his grandeur, and confused by the noise of the trumpets that kept playing incessantly down below. He gazed, half sadly, up to the skylight, whence there came pouring a stream of sunrays, with innumerable motes floating there, like a bridge thrown between heaven and earth. Sliding down it, as if she had been made of air, came the little old woman in gray.

So beautiful looked she—old as she was—that Prince Dolor was at first quite startled by the apparition. Then he held out his arms in eager delight.

"Oh, Godmother, you have not forsaken me!"

"Not at all, my son. You may have not seen me, but I have seen you many a time."

"How?"

"Oh, never mind. I can turn into anything I please, you know. And I have been a bearskin rug and a crystal goblet—and sometimes I have changed from inanimate to animate nature, put on feathers, and made myself very comfortable as a bird."

"Ha!" laughed the prince, a new light breaking in upon him, as he caught the inflection of her tone, lively and mischievous. "Ha, ha! a lark, for instance?"

"Or a magpie," answered she, with a wonderful imitation of Mistress Mag's croaky voice. "Do you suppose I am always sentimental and never funny? If anything makes you happy, gay or grave, don't you think it is more than likely to come through your old godmother?"

"I believe that," said the boy tenderly, holding out his arms. They clasped one another in a close embrace.

Suddenly Prince Dolor looked very anxious. "You will not leave me now that I am a king? Otherwise, I had rather not be a king at all. Promise never to forsake me?"

The little old woman laughed gaily. "Forsake you? That is impossible. But it is just possible you may forsake me. Not probable though. Your mother never did, and she was a queen. The sweetest queen in all the world was the Lady Dolorez."

"Tell me about her," said the boy eagerly. "As I get older I think I can understand more. Do tell me."

"Not now. You couldn't hear me for the trumpets and the shouting.

Hope Dunlap '09

But when you come to the palace, ask for a long-closed upper room, which looks out upon the Beautiful Mountains. Open it and take it for your own. Whenever you go there, you will always find me, and we will talk together about all sorts of things."

"And about my mother?"

The little old woman nodded and kept nodding and smiling to herself many times, as the boy repeated over and over again the sweet words he had never known or understood—"my mother—my mother."

"Now I must go," said she, as the trumpets blared louder and louder, and the shouts of the people showed that they would not endure any delay. "Good-bye, Good-bye! Open the window and out I fly."

Prince Dolor repeated gaily the musical rhyme, but all the while tried to hold his godmother fast.

Vain, vain! For the moment that a knocking was heard at his door, the sun went behind a cloud, the bright stream of dancing motes vanished, and the little old woman with them, he knew not where.

So Prince Dolor left his tower—which he had entered so mournfully and ignominously, as a little helpless baby carried in the deaf man's arms—left it as the great king of Nomansland.

The only thing he took away with him was something so insignificant that none of the lords, gentlemen, and soldiers who escorted him with such triumphant splendor could possibly notice it. It was a tiny bundle, which he had found lying on the floor just where the bridge of sunbeams had rested. At once he had pounced upon it, and thrust it secretly into his shirt, where it dwindled into such small proportions, that it might have been taken for a bit of flannel or an old pocket handkerchief!

It was his traveling cloak.

Chapter Ten

Prince Dolor made an excellent king. Nobody ever does anything less well, not even the commonest duty of common daily life, for having such a godmother as the little old woman clothed in gray. Nor is anybody less good, less capable of both work and enjoyment later in life, for having been a little unhappy in his youth, as the prince had been.

Whenever people worried and bothered him—as they did sometimes, with state etiquette, state squabbles, and the like, setting up themselves and pulling down their neighbors—he would take refuge in the upper room that looked out on the Beautiful Mountains and, laying his head on his godmother's shoulder, become calmed and at rest.

Also, she helped him out of any difficulty that now and then occurred, for there never was such a wise old woman. When the people of Nomansland raised the alarm—as sometimes they did—for what people can exist without a little fault-finding?—and began to cry out, "Unhappy is the nation whose king is a child," she would say to him gently, "You are a child. Accept the fact. Be humble. Be teachable. Lean upon the wisdom of others until you have gained your own."

He did so. He learned how to take advice before attempting to give it, to obey before he could righteously command. He assembled around him all the good and wise of his kingdom. He laid all its affairs before them, and was guided by their opinions until he had formed his own.

This he did, sooner than anybody would have imagined who did not know of his godmother and his traveling cloak—two secret blessings, which, though many guessed at, nobody quite understood. Nor did they understand why he loved so the little upper room, except that it had been his mother's room, from the window of which, as people remembered now, she used to sit for hours watching the Beautiful Mountains.

Out of that window he used to fly—not very often. As he grew older, the labor of state prevented the frequent use of his traveling cloak. Still he did use it sometimes. Only now it was less for his own pleasure and amusement than to see something, or investigate something, for the good of the country. But he prized his godmother's gift as dearly as ever. It was a comfort to him in all his vexations, an enhancement of all his joys. It made him almost forget his lameness, which was never cured.

However, the cruel things that had been once foreboded of him did not happen. His misfortune was not such a heavy one after all. It proved to be much less inconvenience, even to himself, than had been feared. A council of eminent surgeons and mechanicians invented for him a wonderful pair of crutches, with the help of which, though he never walked easily or gracefully, he did manage to walk, so as to be quite independent. And such was the love his people bore him that they never heard the sound of his crutches on the marble palace floors without a leap of the heart, for they knew that good was coming to them whenever he approached them.

Thus, though he never walked in processions, never reviewed his troops mounted on a magnificent charger, nor did any of the things that make a show monarch so much appreciated, he was able for all the duties and a great many of the pleasures of his rank. When he held his audiences, not standing, but seated on a throne, ingeniously contrived to hide his infirmity, the people thronged to greet him. When he drove out through the city streets, shouts followed him wherever he went. Faces brightened as he passed, and his own, perhaps, was the brightest of all.

First, because, accepting his affliction as inevitable, he took it patiently. Second, because, being a brave man, he bore it bravely; trying to forget himself, and live out of himself, and in and for other people. Therefore other people grew to love him so well that hundreds of his subjects might have been found who were almost ready to die for their lame king.

He never gave them a queen. When they implored him to choose one, he replied that his country was his bride, and he desired no other. But, perhaps, the real reason was that he shrank from any change; and that no wife in all the world would have been found so perfect, so lovable, so tender to him in all his weaknesses, as his beautiful old godmother.

His four-and-twenty other godfathers and godmothers, or as many of them as were still alive, crowded round him as soon as he ascended the throne. He was very civil to them all, but adopted none of the names they had given him, keeping to the one by which he had been always known, though it had now almost lost its meaning, for King Dolor was one of the happiest and most cheerful men alive.

He did a good many things, however, unlike most men and most kings, which a little astonished his subjects. First, he pardoned the condemned woman who had been his nurse, and ordained that from henceforward there should be no such thing as the punishment of death in Nomansland. All capital criminals were to be sent to perpetual imprisonment in Hopeless Tower, and the plain round about it, where they could do no harm to anybody, and might in time do a little good, as the woman had done.

Another surprise he shortly afterward gave the nation. He recalled his uncle's family, who had fled away in terror to another country, and restored them to all their honors in their own. By and by he chose the eldest son of his eldest cousin (who had been dead a year), and had him educated in the royal palace, as the heir to the throne. This little prince was a quiet, unobtrusive boy, so that everybody wondered at the king's choosing him, when there were so many more. But as he grew into a fine young fellow, good and brave, they agreed that the king judged more wisely than they.

"Not a lame prince neither," His Majesty observed one day, watching him affectionately, for he was the best runner, the highest leaper, the keenest and most active sportsman in the country. "One cannot make oneself, but one can sometimes help a little in the making of somebody else. It is well."

This was said, not to any of his great lords and ladies, but to a good old woman—his first nurse—whom he had sought for far and wide, and at last found in her cottage among the Beautiful Mountains. He sent for her to visit him once a year, and treated her with great honor until she died. He was equally kind, though somewhat less tender, to his other nurse, who, after receiving her pardon, returned to her native town and grew into a lady, and a good one.

Thus King Dolor's reign passed, year after year, long and prosperous. Whether he was happy—"as happy as a king"—is a question no human being can decide. But he probably was, because he had the power of making everybody about him happy, and did it too. Also because he was his godmother's godson, and could shut himself up with her whenever he liked, in that quiet little room, in view of the Beautiful Mountains, which nobody else ever saw or cared to see. They were too far off, and the city lay so low. But there they were, all the time. They never changed; and, at any day throughout his long reign, the king would sooner have lost his crown than have lost sight of the Beautiful Mountains.

In course of time, when the little prince, his cousin, was grown into a tall young man, capable of all the duties of a man, His Majesty did one of the most extraordinary acts ever known in a sovereign beloved by his people and prosperous in his reign. He announced that he wished to invest his heir with the royal purple—at any rate, for a time—while he himself went away on a distant journey, to a place he had long desired to go.

Everybody marveled, but nobody opposed him. Who could oppose the good king, who was not a young king now? And, besides, the nation had a great admiration for the young regent—and, possibly, a lurking pleasure in change.

So there was fixed a day, when all the people whom it would hold, assembled in the great square of the capital, to see the young prince installed solemnly in his new duties, and undertaking his new vows. He was a very fine young fellow, tall and straight as a poplar tree, with a frank, handsome face—a great deal handsomer than the king, some people said, but others thought differently. However, as His Majesty sat on his throne, with his gray hair falling from underneath his crown, and a few wrinkles showing in spite of his smile, there was something about

H·D·

his countenance that made his people, even while they shouted, regard him with a tenderness mixed with awe.

He lifted up his thin, slender hand, and there came a silence over the vast crowd immediately. Then he spoke, in his own accustomed way, using no grand words, but saying what he had to say in the simplest fashion, though with a clearness that struck their ears like the first song of a bird in the dusk of the morning.

"My people, I am tired. I want to rest. I have had a long reign, and done much work—at least, as much as I was able to do. Many might have done it better than I, but none with a better will. Now I leave it to others. I am tired, very tired. Let me go home."

There rose a murmur—of content and discontent none could well tell. Then it died down again, and the assembly listened silently once more.

"I am not anxious about you—my people—my children," continued the king. "You are prosperous and at peace. I leave you in good hands. The prince regent will be a fitter king for you than I."

"No, no, no!" rose the universal shout—and those who had sometimes found fault with him shouted louder than anybody. But he seemed as if he heard them not.

"Yes, yes," said he, as soon as the tumult had a little subsided, and his voice sounded firm and clear. And some very old people, who boasted of having seen him as a child, declared that his face took a sudden change, and grew as young and sweet as that of the little Prince Dolor. "Yes, I must go. It is time for me to go. Remember me sometimes, my people, for I have loved you well. And I am going a long way, and I do not think I shall come back any more."

He drew a little bundle out of his breast pocket—a bundle that nobody had ever seen before. It was small and shabby-looking, and tied up with many knots, which untied themselves in an instant. With a joyful countenance, he muttered over it a few half-intelligible words. Then, so suddenly that even those nearest to His Majesty could not tell how it came about, the king was away—away—floating right up in the air—upon something, they knew not what, except that it appeared to be as safe and pleasant as the wings of a bird.

And after him sprang a bird, a dear little lark, rising from where no one could say, since larks do not usually build their nests in the pavement of city squares. But there it was, a real lark, singing far over their heads, louder and clearer, and more joyful, as it flew further into the blue sky.

Shading their eyes, and straining their ears, the astonished people stood, until the whole vision disappeared like a speck in the clouds, the rosy clouds that overhung the Beautiful Mountains.

Then they guessed that they should see their beloved king no more. Well-beloved as he was, he had always been somewhat of a mystery to them, and such he remained. But they went home, and, accepting their new monarch, obeyed him faithfully for his cousin's sake.

King Dolor was never again beheld or heard of in his own country. But the good he had done there lasted for years and years. He was long missed and deeply mourned—at least, so far as anybody could mourn one who was gone on such a happy journey.

Where he went, or who went with him, it is impossible to say. But perhaps his godmother took him, on his traveling cloak, to the Beautiful Mountains. What he did there, or where he is now, who can tell? But certainly, wherever he is, he is perfectly happy.